PRAISE FOR *KRAMPUSNACHT*

"A kaleidoscope of Krampus tales featuring enjoyable twists and turns. Imaginative and entertaining."
— Monte Beauchamp, *Krampus: The Devil of Christmas*

"Twelve enthralling tales that turn the lights out on Christmas, and dance with folklore in the dark."
— Kristina Wojtaszek, author of *Opal*

Krampusnacht

Twelve Nights of Krampus

Edited by
KATE WOLFORD

World Weaver Press

KRAMPUSNACHT: TWELVE NIGHTS OF KRAMPUS
Copyright © 2014 Kate Wolford

Published by World Weaver Press
Alpena, Michigan
www.WorldWeaverPress.com

Cover illustration by Searing Limb / Connor Anderson
Cover layout by World Weaver Press
Publishing Editor: Eileen Wiedbrauk

First Edition: November 2014

ISBN: 0692314741
ISBN-13: 978-0692314746

Also available as an ebook.

KRAMPUSNACHT

KRAMPUSNACHT

INTRODUCTION

Kate Wolford

We live in an age of the antihero. Millions worship at the bright blue altar of Walter White, meth and myth maker, whose reign as the best worst TV protagonist shows no sign of diminishing even though *Breaking Bad* is over. And, chances are, should you be a Harry Potter fan, you were far more interested in the fate of Severus Snape than that of Harry. *Game of Thrones*, which bestrides the world of entertainment like some giant straight out of George R.R. Martin's imagination, has no true, pure characters over the age of ten.

Is it any wonder, then, that an old, dark figure, complete with horns, hoofs, and an utterly terrifying tongue, not to mention a penchant for discipline (torture?), is emerging into pop culture in the U.S.?

His name is Krampus. And this volume contains 12 stories featuring him as villain, savior, lover, dupe, and much more. But first, let's investigate the cloven hoofed gentleman who is a companion to "The Right Jolly Old Elf."

In case Krampus is new to you, here's an important thing you need to know: His origins are lost in time. Be suspicious of any source purporting to tell you the "true" story of him.

To begin, let's take a look at him: He's easy to find. Images of Krampus are all over the Internet. He'll always have horns—usually long and curled—so perhaps his origins can be traced back to the Greek God Pan. Pan, like Krampus, has hoofs and horns and was a wild thing of nature. Krampus, no matter how he is dressed in art or literature, is wild. (According to *National Geographic Daily News*, his name comes from *krampen*, which meant "claw" in German—other sources suggest it's from older High German for claw. Claws can be pretty wild.) He's animalistic, usually shown with a furry body and tail. His hideously long tongue is a bit like a snake's and, like Satan, he brings the dark into the "Eden" people usually wish Christmas to be.

In fact, Krampus, or, "the Krampus," is sometimes known as "The Christmas Devil" and like Satan, he is the dark, demonic, disturbing opposite of holy light. But the Krampus tradition does not represent the struggle between good and evil. Traditionally, Krampus is kind of a companion to St. Nicholas, not his adversary. Think of him as Santa's Enforcer. For old lore has it that Krampus metes out justice to brats who deserve not toys and games but rather a good thrashing with Krampus' *ruten*, which is a bunch of twigs or branches. Truly, deeply, horrible children might get chained and dragged to Hell (or put in a giant basket and hauled to the same destination). Krampus and Hell have something of a history, according to *National Geographic Daily News* and other sources, which assert that Krampus is the son of Hel, who in Norse mythology is a kind of empress of the Land of the Dead.

(Maybe Krampus just wants lots of people at the table when he goes home to visit mom for the holidays, and that's why he snatches up those kids. Probably not.)

Intriguingly nasty folklore, isn't it? And just where did it come from? Saint Nick has a companion in many countries, especially in Europe, and Krampus is just one example of these. Krampus has long been popular in countries such as Germany, Austria, and Northern Italy. According to Krampus.com, "Home of the Christmas Devil," an excellent source of all things Krampus, "The European practice of *mummery* during the winter solstice season can be traced back tens of thousands of years. Villagers across the continent dress up as animals, wild-men and mythic figures to parade and perform humorous plays. This ancient guising and masking tradition continues to this day [in

Halloween costuming and celebrations].” Krampus, then, feels new to most people in the U.S., but he's very old news to millions of people in Europe. He springs from the old pagan ways of the village, forest, and field in old cultures of old peoples.

Krampusnacht is usually held on the Eve of Saint Nicholas Day, the latter of which remains a popular festival for families, and especially children, throughout Europe. The Night of Krampus is held on December 5, while the joyous, light, happy holiday of Saint Nicholas is held on December 6, when children enjoy treats, often found in stockings or shoes—the tradition directly connected to “hanging stockings with care” on Christmas Eve. But Krampusnacht, well, that is quite a different story. People dressed like Krampus or some other scary, folkloric figure, make a Krampus Run or*Krampuslauf.* Booze seems to play a big role in many of these celebrations, and the rowdiness and general mayhem seem to have, traditionally and currently, scared bystanders of all ages. Not surprisingly, not all parents are Krampus fans in countries where he is celebrated. Pictures of the revelry might give you a shiver of something dark, old, and more than little unholy—no matter how gentle and pedestrian the people inside those costume likely are 364 days of the year. Think of some of the worst villains, witches, and goblins in fairy tales, and you've got the idea of the revelry and scariness than can happen on Krampusnacht. (Although, to be clear, none of my research suggests that Krampus revelers are out to actually hurt kids.)

Over here, in the U.S. (and in much of the rest of the English-speaking world), Krampus has been on the down low for, well, forever. Our traditions, strongly influenced by Charles Dickens' *A Christmas Carol* and Clement Clarke Moore's “A Visit from St. Nicholas,” largely focus on Christmas, and especially Saint Nick or Santa Claus. Here in the States, despite threats of lumps of coal, Santa's companions are elves who slave happily for him up in the North Pole. Everybody loves Santa. He has no dark companions or dark side. (Unless you count the terrible way he treats Rudolph in *Rudolph the Red Nosed Reindeer,* the

TV special. And I do count it. I really, really do. Santa doesn't like difference.)

Doubtless, families in the U.S. with German heritage have kept Krampus alive. But most people here and in Canada, the U.K., and other English-speaking countries where Christmas is celebrated, began to be aware of Krampus a few years ago. Indeed, research about Krampus suggests that most people are only now dimly aware of him as part of Christmas lore, if they've heard of him at all. But nonetheless, the Krampus has arrived.

Why now? Why, in the last decade has Krampus leapt from the Alpine Region of Europe to cities like Los Angeles, Bloomington, IN; Seattle; and Edmonton, Canada? All of those cities now have Krampus celebrations. And the Internet is now awash in Krampus. You can find countless images of Krampus from the late 19th century through the early 20th, when *Krampkarten* were especially popular. And, for the last few years, major news outlets have been doing Krampus stories, so media is spreading the message. But that doesn't fully explain why Krampus is catching on so successfully in countries like the U.S.

Maybe, just maybe, we've had enough of treacly Santa Claus, whose heart is supposedly so big and full of love for all children that he's compelled to break into their houses and leave them toys. Maybe it's because people are so sick to death of coddled kids who aren't allowed to play outside and blow off steam, so they scream it off in restaurants, and are, as a result, in need of a Krampus corrective. Maybe it's because parents are sick of leaving milk and cookies for Santa and would rather leave beer and sausage for Krampus. (As far as I know, Krampus doesn't have such a preference, but I bet he'd like beer and sausage.) And maybe parents in countries like the U.S. are sick of the lack of balance in our secular Christmas celebrations. Maybe they've realized that threatening to text Santa with reports of bad behavior just doesn't do the job, and it's time to release some old European justice—even if it's all imaginary. And let's face it, kids over six are going to go for

Krampus big time. Kids love creepy, scary stuff. He has the potential to put the cool back into the Yule.

So there you have it: Fantastical images, an excuse for mayhem and partying, a celebration of the old folkways, and a chance to start new family traditions. Krampus is offering us all of that, and a lot of the world is listening. Plus, he's clearly antihero material. Krampus just screams out for stories that show you his potential for narrative surprises and character twists. In this book, a dozen writers have plumbed the depths of Krampus lore and their own imaginations to bring you an array of stories that range from sly to terrifying to sweet to funny. There's a lot of payback and justice in this book, and some of it is directed at kids and adults and some of it is directed at Krampus. You'll see, by their notes on inspiration, that Krampus rampaged through these writers' imaginations. In this collection, you'll find:

"Prodigious": A pretty cool guy named Brian has a truly transformative Krampus experience.

"The Wicked Child": Krampus helps a lonely, rejected little girl find her true path.

"Marching Krampus": A rotten brother gets some Krampus justice.

"Peppermint Sticks": A down-on-his-luck guy takes a job with Krampus. It proves to be a tough gig.

"Ring, Little Bell, Ring": Krampus is a lover and a lawman in a strange little town.

"A Visit": This story has an old-fashioned setting, and tremendous buildup toward a faceoff with Krampus.

"Santa Claus and the Girl Who Loved to Sing and Dance": He tussles with a monstrous child who won't let Santa or anyone else get in the way of stardom.

"Between the Eyes": The Horned One walks into a bar and wreaks hell on the life of an unwitting victim.

"Nothing to Dread": The Christmas Devil is well and truly caught by a little boy.

"Raw Recruits": Krampus runs a sweatshop. In Hell.

"The God Killer": Krampus is stalked. Things get choppy.

"A Krampus Carol": There really, truly is a "get off my lawn" story of Krampus in these pages. And just who's the bad guy here?

Unwrap these little "presents" all at once or one by one. You'll see all sides of Krampus and the holidays. I've enjoyed discovering them and putting this collection together, and hope you'll love these stories as much as I do. And remember, if you're inclined to listen for footsteps on the roof on Christmas Eve, don't just expect the thump of a boot. Keep your ears open for the clip-clop of hoofs, the rattle of chains and the whoosh of a ruten.

Enjoy the holidays.

Kate Wolford
Editor, *Krampusnacht*

The First Night of Krampus:

PRODIGIOUS

Elizabeth Twist

Inspiration: Elizabeth first learned about Krampus through Monte Beauchamp's beautifully curated collection of Krampus postcards, *The Devil in Design*. In addition to the numerous images of Krampus hauling away naughty children, she noticed there's another theme running through the collection: Krampus wooing cute women. "Prodigious" is based on the notion of a Krampus who longs for romance.

Sweet Gwendolyn's voice calls to me across Super Fun Toy Super Store. "Brian! Come here!"

For a moment my heart and nethers flutter. She's going to ask me to a Christmas party and kiss me lightly, then passionately, under the mistletoe. Or maybe not, but I can dream.

Between me and Gwendolyn stand twin boys pelting each other with hard rubber balls. A baby girl has fallen on her bottom trying to toddle after her big brother who, based on her shrieks, is named Peter. He scowls and points and laughs as he whips stuffed dinosaurs at her head. Some children are naturally worse than others but I don't care; I catch a glimpse of Gwendolyn standing by the staff room door.

A tot catches my pant leg, smearing me with what I can only hope is chocolate. I plastic smile down at him. A woman tugs my sleeve. She's covered in let's-hope-it's-chocolate too.

"Excuse me," she says. "Where's the washroom? Thomas needs a diaper change."

I gesture wildly and give instructions and extract myself from their sticky embrace. She doesn't so much as thank me.

One of Gwendolyn's porcelain hands is resting on the door handle to freedom, for beyond the staff room door is the locker room that holds our coats and car keys, and from there it's one more door out to the back parking lot. I imagine we won't say a word as we rush out to my car and maybe drive a block or two before we pull over and do to each other what we are clearly meant to do.

"What's up?" I'm playing it cool. The only time we've ever done anything is in my imagination. I recognize that.

She smiles. Her brunette curls bounce and shine over her perfect shoulders and she says perfect words: "I need you out back."

I bet you do. I can't—and don't—say that out loud. "Need help with something?"

She nods, and opens the door. My heart jumps into my esophagus and performs a tango. She takes her coat from her locker. "Cold out there. You'll want your coat too."

Adding more clothes to the situation is not what I want, but she's right; it's freezing outside. We bundle up and she opens the door, and I can't believe I get to spend time with her. Payne has never been anything but nice to me. He goes out of his way to pretend our jobs are important, and he always asks how I'm doing and remembers my name and everything, but I swear he sets up our shifts so Gwendolyn and I are never together.

The back parking lot, normally containing a few staff cars, is crowded with people. It looks like everyone who works for the store is here, arranging lawn furniture and wrapping things in red and green paper and making piles of glittery cotton "snow." They're hammering together a small train track and assembling a plywood stage with a foil-wrapped arch on it that says "Santa Claus."

The Christmas party is tomorrow night. With the rush inside the store, I'd forgotten.

Mr. Payne waves us over. His red cheeks make him look like a Campbell's soup kid. He thumbs his suspenders—he wears them even when he's not about to play Santa—and yells Gwendolyn's name magnanimously even though we're only a few feet away. He follows it up with a few ho ho ho's.

She laughs. "Pretty good," she says. She has to say that, though. He's her dad.

"Well?" Payne asks. He looks at me expectantly. I smile. I'm coming in partway through the conversation.

Gwendolyn smiles at me. It's enough to make me swoon, but I still don't know what all this is about.

"Stick out your tongue," she says.

I freeze. My tongue is my thing.

Everybody has a thing. You can wiggle your ears or turn your eyelids inside out or flare your nostrils. You're double jointed or have a weird birthmark shaped like a hand or a bunny or a something. Your thing.

One of my deepest regrets, second only to the fact that I work at a place called Super Fun Toy Super Store, is that two weeks after I started here, this past January, I attended a staff party at which I got way too drunk. I was trying to impress a girl. Okay, it was Jeannie from the stock room. This was before I met Gwendolyn. Anyway, I popped my eyes open and stuck out my tongue at her.

If you ever have the misfortune to get a job at Super Fun Toy Super Store, "Have you seen Brian's tongue?" is the question they will ask you *before* they ask if you know how to work a cash register.

"Come on," Gwendolyn says. "Stick out your tongue. Daddy wants to see it."

Ice devours my heart and I stick out my tongue.

"See?" Gwendolyn says. "It's perfect, right?"

Mr. Payne frowns. I tuck my tongue back behind my teeth. It's long enough that I know it looks like it shouldn't fit. It does.

The frown melts into a smile and Payne howls, not the fake ho-ho of a toy store Santa, but a this-is-gonna-be-good laugh of a frat boy planning a week of hazing. Hey, if he's happy, I'm happy, but still. It's disconcerting.

"All right!" Payne wipes tears away. "I can honestly say I've never seen anything like it. He's perfect. Just like you said, honey."

Gwendolyn's squee fills the parking lot. The busy worker bees pause in their hammering and wrapping and lift their heads for a moment, then drop them when they see Payne standing there, smiles playing on their faces. Everybody's mood seems to lift when Payne is around. He's always laughing and making a joke, but never at anybody's expense. Not until today, anyway.

To say this is awkward doesn't come close to covering it. I don't love my job, but Payne is pretty much my favorite of all the bosses I've had, and somehow the girl of my dreams has just exposed me to something that feels a whole lot like a weirdly sexual medical exam. There has to be some explanation.

"Brian, this year you're going to play Krampus! Gwendolyn and I insist."

"Uh." I manage. "What's a Krampus?"

* * *

Payne's second-in-command, Lennox, takes me into the storage room behind the staff locker room, her high, tight ponytail waving in my face. She flips through the substantial collection of keys on her key ring, selects one, and uses it to open *the door*.

The door is the weirdest thing. It's located in the back of the broom closet, where you wouldn't think a door would be. No one I've talked to has ever seen *the door* open, not even once, in the almost-year that I have worked here.

Don't cross Lennox is one of the first rules you learn here. That she has a key to *the door* is one of many signs of her power.

My running theory, that *the door* is a secret access to Narnia, is finally put to rest as she pulls the chain on the single ancient light bulb dangling from the ceiling. My first impression is that the room is full of furs: I see empty skins hanging, and there's a musky smell. Then I catch a glimpse of red velvet trimmed in white and I realize: costumes. They're hanging from pegs and hooks and hangers, elaborately rigged for each outfit.

It all makes a kind of sense now: There is the white bunny outfit that Ken wore at Easter. There's the greasy black wig, pointed hat, and green hooked warty nose that Shelley wore at Halloween, and the turkey costume Alex dressed in just a few weeks ago for the Thanksgiving! Blowout! Sale!

I stare at the Santa outfit. It seems custom made for someone bigger than most of the staffers. On the floor beside it sits a pair of soft black leather boots. I reach out to touch one.

"Better not," Lennox says. Her tone is so peculiar I turn and stare at her. She wears a sneer that I can only describe as "triumphant."

It's Christmas, though. "Isn't this for me? You know, for the party?" Krampus could be a word for Santa, in some language. Even as I think it, I know that's probably not right.

Her laugh is hideous. I remember I turned her down, back in January, when she shyly asked me if I wanted to see a movie with her. Then I told a couple of the other girls on staff. I have a big mouth sometimes. Lennox hates me. She's loving this.

My voice only squeaks a little as I ask, "So if I'm not Santa, then who am I supposed to be?"

There's an elf costume to the right of the Santa outfit, but Lennox points to the back of the long, narrow room, at a rough, brown-furred thing hanging where the light doesn't quite manage to penetrate. I go to it, as to my doom.

The thick smell of animal skins I detected from the doorway originates from this costume. I pull it out from the wall and for a moment I think I'm looking at a disheveled coat sewn entirely from wolves' hackles—the fur is that long, that spikey. As I examine it, I see it's a onesie, having pants and top with holes for the hands, feet, and head, and access granted by a row of large wooden toggles down the front.

A flexible mask—skin, I think, not rubber—hangs from a peg nearby. It's hideous, a flapping devil's face with a gaping open mouth. An ancient bottle of spirit gum hangs beside it from a bit of string. There's no elastic to hold the mask on. I'll have to glue it to my face.

The costume comes with a single awkward looking shoe. "There's only one," Lennox says. "Krampus has one cloven hoof and one human foot. The foot is bare." She finishes with a smirk.

"Help me out here," I say, genuinely scared at the prospect of wearing this thing, although I couldn't say why.

"You know how Santa is supposed to leave lumps of coal in your stocking if you're naughty?"

I nod.

"Let's say it isn't Santa. Let's say Santa only wants to deal with nice kids. Somebody still has to deliver the coal."

"Krampus."

"Krampus." She pops her gum as if that's the last word.

I take the costume down off its hook and drape it over my arm. I clutch the shoe, mask, and glue bottle in one hand. I'm about to leave the costume closet, which Lennox is waiting to lock, but she stops me.

"You forgot that stuff. That's yours too."

In the back corner I find a thing like a three foot long whisk made of sticks and a giant curving pair of ram's horns that look like they've been torn directly from the animal. Shreds of fur and dried skin stick to the flat ends. A strange harness attaches them together. There's also a bushel basket with straps so you can wear it like a backpack. It's all too weird.

Lennox tells me I've got the rest of the afternoon to go home and prepare. On my way out the door, I pause.

"Who's playing Santa Claus?"

Lennox rolls her eyes. "Who do you think?"

Fear has made me utterly stupid. "You?"

She laughs and shakes her head. Her ponytail swishes like it's got anger of its own. "The big guy, dummy."

I don't quite stop myself from saying "God?" I know who she's talking about. Of course it's Payne.

* * *

I park a few blocks away from the store, so no one who's likely to attend the party will see me struggle into the horns or strap the bushel basket onto my back. I've spent the afternoon at my apartment, practicing threatening poses in front of a full-length mirror, the one legacy of my last girlfriend.

The Krampus gear looks awesome, if I do say so myself. The fur outfit is a little more like a weird coat than a costume, but the mask and the horns more than make up for it. I'm eight feet tall with all of it put together, and when my prodigious tongue sticks out through the rubbery black lips of the mask, it's magic. I look truly demonic. For once I'm okay with the fact that my mom is dead, I never knew my dad, and I don't have any living family that I know of. It makes for a bummer of a holiday season, but maybe I can be different, maybe there's room for a demon in the story of Christmas, and maybe that's my place.

Once I'm all strapped in, I grab the giant whisk thing, and I set off for the parking lot.

By this point I've figured out how to walk with just the one hoof. It's actually a clever rig that fits over a tennis shoe. The other foot is supposed to be bare. Hard-core Krampus imitators use shoe polish and nothing else, but it's below freezing, so I'm wearing a brown knitted slipper with individual toes and a patch of leather on the sole, kind of a glove for your foot. It's one of a pair that my mom gave me, a million Christmases ago, before she got sick.

I'm only sort of limping as I cross the parking lot. I snort and show my teeth as I pass the first bunch of kids. They stare.

An older girl, about eight, points. "Mom, what's that?"

Not missing a beat, the woman replies, "Where the wild things are, honey."

I feel an immediate, irrational bout of rage. Not everything is reducible to a famous kid's book or a movie franchise.

I bend down to talk to the little girl. I'm pretty sure she gets a good whiff of the costume: it's earthy and gamey and a little like smoked meat. "I'm Santa's helper," I growl. "You might not know me, but I know you. I hope you've been good, or I might have to take you where all the bad children go."

The girl looks at her mom.

"That's terrible," her mother says. "Do you even work for the store?"

I don't break character. "It's a European tradition," I say, in my creepy-scary monster voice. "I'm Krampus."

The woman breaks into a smile. "Oh! Like Zwart Piet! I'm Dutch."

I have no idea what she's talking about, so I flash my tongue at her and growl.

She claps her hands. "Wonderful!" She pushes her daughter toward me. "It's okay, honey. You've been good this year, but maybe some of these other kids haven't." She winks at me.

Snow starts to fall as I spot Gwendolyn. She's wearing a red velvet coat that follows the curve of her waist. It's trimmed in white and for a second I wonder if Payne has gotten progressive and cast a female Santa. I imagine her walking me through the crowd of kids on a Krampus leash, and then I realize that's a little too fetishy and won't happen—except it could happen later in the privacy of my apartment.

She sees me and puts her hands over her mouth. Realistically speaking, what I'm wearing shouldn't work. The straps should be slipping and the horns falling and the costume chafing, but it all holds. It feels like it's part of me, like it is me.

I stick my tongue out and hiss.

"You look amazing!" Gwendolyn says. "Lennox, doesn't he look amazing?"

Lennox, in her green elf costume, sneers.

When Gwendolyn kisses me, she kisses my lips and the border of the mask.

Payne's heavy hand clamps down on my shoulder just as I pull back to study sweet Gwendolyn's face. He spins me and I'm looking into the frightfully jolly, boiling red face of St. Nick. Behind him, Lennox smirks. I don't know what she's so smug about. Payne likes me and will probably ignore the fact that I was just smooching his daughter.

"You've got a show to put on, Brian," Payne roars in a Santa Clausy tone that puts my creepy-scary monster voice to shame. Together we walk into the crowd and up onto the platform where Santa's throne sits.

Payne yells "Ho Ho Ho" at the kids and their parents until they stop talking and focus on us. I didn't feel it before now, but a solemnity emanates from him that I've never felt before. The smiles fall off the crowd's faces. I develop a sudden new respect for Payne: he has charisma, something I've only got in my tongue. He begins to speak, and I can't focus on the words; the words don't matter. He's talking about tradition but I feel as though I'm teetering on the cusp of ages, on the gauzy film of modernity that shields us from our deep and creepy past. I feel the spiky fur of my body stand up all over. I stamp my hoof and it makes an impossible clopping sound on the particle board stage.

Payne tells the crowd about Krampus while I snarl and giggle malevolently. I smack my clawed hand with the birch switch. I'm ready.

ELIZABETH TWIST

I start scanning the crowd and all I can focus on are the kids. I'm seeing kids for the first time for what they really are: rotten little adults *in potentia*. I want to crush the rottenness from them. I want them to think twice about becoming mean-spirited jerks. They stare back at me. None of them are seeing a Maurice Sendak ripoff now. They're seeing their one natural enemy. I expect they'll start crying but they don't. They're still. They're waiting.

Payne is done talking. I look into his eyes. I've always thought they were brown but right now they're blue and sparkling, a jolly St. Nick blue. He nods, the smallest movement. I race out into the crowd with a speed that surprises even me.

The next few minutes are pure chaos. The kids run from me like a vast school of tiny fish fleeing before a shark. A few of them seem to glow with a wicked red aura. They are mine. I know it. They know it.

The parents are into it. They're cheering and clapping. I see a couple of them push their kids back into my path, as if they *want* me to catch them. It's glorious.

One by one, kids fall panting into fake snow banks or into their parents' arms, shrieking with laughter. On my final round through the parking lot I see Lennox handing out candy canes and small toys. I wonder if that isn't Payne's job, but I catch a glimpse of him on his throne. He's watching me. I can't read the look on his face. It doesn't matter. All I care about is the dance of terror I'm performing with the few remaining kids.

The bad seeds, the ones with the red glow, sweep as a small flock out past the margins of the parking lot into a wooded area I've never noticed before. It's a forest of pine trees. Somehow, they're decorated with tinsel and colored lights that multiply our shadows and throw them in all directions. One of the children, a boy, turns and looks at me as he runs, a grimace of pure malice on his face. He trips and falls.

I don't slow down as I scoop him up and toss him into the basket on my back. I feel his weight back there but I don't mind. I know, somehow, that all the kids will fit if they have to.

22

When we arrive at the hellhole, the rest of the kids are hiding in nearby trees. I can feel their anticipation. They want to know what I'm going to do with their fallen comrade. I admit I'm curious too.

The hole is ringed with rocks. Heat blasts out of it along with a red light that glows dark and dull, seeming to absorb the light from the trees rather than add to it. I peer down into it. The fire is full of writhing masses: body parts, tentacles, chthonic mysteries I wish I'd never laid eyes on.

I want to take the little monster on my back and dump him in. I pluck him from the basket and hold him in my claws. I stick my tongue out and he's silent, solemn, as stunned and docile as any mouse on the verge of death by cat.

I want to throw him in. Something makes me stop. That something is me. I'm remembering stuff, specifically, all the crappy things I did as a kid. Even though I'm not good all the time now, I try. I grew up. I got better.

I'm not done yet. I get lots of chances. Maybe this kid deserves that too. Hell, maybe what's happening right now will help him change.

I put him down. He scrambles over to where the other kids are hiding and scoots into the underbrush. Their eyes peer out at me.

The horns slip off my head. I just barely catch them before they fall into the hole. I step back from it. I'm suddenly conscious of my tee shirt and jeans under the heavy Krampus costume. I look at my hands. They're just my hands in brown gloves: no claws.

"It's okay kids," I say to the children in hiding. "Come out. Let's go get some candy."

"You can't fool them. It's not okay and it's not over."

Payne stands behind me, still in his Santa regalia. His hands rest on his hips and he seems to fill the corridor between the trees, my only exit. There's no getting past him. I realize I'm genuinely scared of the flaming hellhole behind me.

"What are you doing?" I ask. I already know the answer but I hope I'm wrong.

He takes a step closer. He casts a quick glance toward the tree under which the kids hide. "I thought for a minute there you were really going to do it."

"I wouldn't," I stammer.

"I know," he says. "Pity. Gwennie had such faith in you."

The air goes out of the world as I begin to realize Payne really was too good to be true. He's not a standard regulation bad boss: he's simply evil. If I step back from him, I'll be too close to the hole for safety. I start talking. It's one way to stall while I figure out how to get away.

"So," I manage. "Ritual sacrifice."

Payne nods. "You think this business runs itself? In this economy? No, to have a real toy store you need real magic." He gestures at the hole. "This is mine."

I take a step to the side. The trees crowd together, shuffling subtly so there's no way through. Real magic is real.

"You'll have to remove the costume," Payne says. "It's an antique, and quite infused with certain . . . properties. I don't want it to burn with you."

"So that's it?" Still stalling. "Krampus is sacrificed?"

"Take. It. Off."

The jolly has come off the Saint Nick. I dawdle as I undo the wooden toggles. I talk quietly.

"If I'd thrown the kid in, then what?"

Payne takes a step or two closer to me. "You'd have been part of the team. Part of the family."

I bend down to undo the strap on the hoof and step out of it. I'm feeling the cold now.

"He didn't do it, did he?" The voice is high-pitched and comes from behind Payne. Lennox. She's here, no doubt, to watch the grand finale.

I wonder if Lennox has played Krampus. I wonder if she sacrificed a child to earn her place on the team.

Gwendolyn steps through the trees behind her. Her eyes are rimmed red and she's sniffling. At least someone feels bad about my imminent demise.

"Gwen," I say. "Please, you can stop this."

She shakes her head. Her expression is hard. "I thought you were meaner. I thought you would do it. Do you know what you've given up?"

I stare at her. I've always thought she was the most beautiful woman, but it's like I'm seeing her for the first time.

She scowls. "You actually became Krampus. That power you had, that strength. It could have been yours forever. I could have been yours." She turns her head away and two perfect tears roll down her cheeks.

I'm still trying to process the idea that Gwen was looking to bone a monster when Payne speaks to me for the last time. "Guess she was wrong." He shrugs. "Oh well."

When he makes his move, I'm ready. He rushes me, hands out in front, aiming a classic shove straight at my chest. I've watched him for a long time, though. You have to watch a guy when you're in love with his daughter. He's top-heavy. I'm channeling all the Kung Fu movies I've ever watched as I grab his red velvet coat and pivot. Instead of moving me, his force carries him around me and forward. I let go just in time for him to pitch into the hole.

A gout of flame spouts up around him, towering ten feet into the air and plunging back down again like a frisky burning porpoise.

On some level, I must be aware of what Lennox is going to do. I step out of the way as she rushes me and she plunges into the hole after her rotten boss.

I figure it's done: two human sacrifices for one.

Gwendolyn surprises me. One moment she's walking toward me, arms outstretched. I've been so in the habit of thinking of her as a gentle, almost fragile beauty that I imagine she only wants to collapse in my arms and thank me. For what, I don't know. The end of the story? Some kind of happily ever after? I just killed her dad, but he was an evil wizard. Thanks for a job well done, then.

I walk into her embrace.

Her hands are around my throat and she's choking the crap out of me. Her grip is surprisingly strong. I struggle to push her hands away, but the best I can do is throw my weight backward and take her off balance. The world goes dark and we fall straight toward the hole and this is not what I wanted, not at all.

We hit the ground hard. Real snow poofs out from under us. We're in the circle of rocks, but the hell hole is gone. Gwendolyn is out cold.

I stand up and dust snow off the costume. I look down at Gwendolyn, at her perfect red lips and her white skin, the white trim on her costume, and for the first time I see that red glow, the same one I saw around the bad kids. She has it. Some people don't grow out of it, I guess.

This is clarity, I realize. Whatever this night has done to me, it's given me something I never had: a way to evaluate people. Oh, it might be crude, but it sure is better than whatever I've been working with up until now.

Despite everything that's happened, I am still completely shocked when I hear the jingle bells ringing in the sky above me. I don't see the sleigh or the reindeer, but all of a sudden *he's* standing in front of me. I expect him to shout Merry Christmas in my face, but he doesn't. He's solemn. A sense of peace breathes out from him. A hush comes over the grove. I shoot a look over to the kids under the trees. They're all fast asleep.

"Hello, Brian."

"Hi Santa."

He snaps his fingers, and five or six tiny men in green outfits scurry out from under the trees. Each one throws a sleeping kid over his shoulder and hurries away, back toward the toy store. Gwendolyn still lies there unconscious, but I'm learning to ignore her.

"They're going to make sure those kids get back to their parents, right?"

"Yes," Santa says. He smiles at me, and it's like the whole magic of the season wraps around me, relaxing every muscle. "They won't remember what they've seen, but let's just say that they might find themselves wanting to be a little bit less naughty from now on."

Santa is a badass.

"You're probably wondering why I'm here, Brian," he says. "The truth is that I haven't been able to come here for some time. Mr. Payne's magic was doing more than making a hole in the world. It was contaminating all levels of this reality. My toy factory hasn't been able to work at full efficiency for three years."

"That's a real thing?" I think about all the toys we sell at Super Fun Toy Super Store. If only parents knew that Santa was giving them away, Payne might have been out of business long before tonight.

Santa reaches into a pocket and pulls out a green and red ball. He hands it to me. It's tiny. I hold it in my palms for a moment. It dissolves in a puff of smoke and I feel an intense rush of joy that doesn't subside. I want to race around the clearing, do a cartwheel. I'm scared that I might hurt myself, though, so I just ride the wave.

"That's a toy," I tell Santa. "Wow."

"It's a type of toy," he says. "You can understand why I want to be able to keep making them. There isn't enough joy in the world. The fact is, people like Payne make what I do next to impossible. I need help, Brian. After the job you did tonight, I think you're an ideal candidate for the position."

The thought of being able to leave the store only adds to the joy I'm feeling. My cup runneth over, and I clap my hands. "What do I have to do?"

Santa pauses, looks me up and down. I get the sense that he's a little reluctant to say this next part. "Well, what I need is a new Krampus. The job fell out of favor with humanity a couple of centuries ago. Sure, there's been an uptick in the popularity of the idea recently, for reasons

I don't completely understand, but people just want to put Krampus on for a night. They don't want to *be* him. They don't really understand about good and evil, or how to distinguish between the two."

"But I was just in costume, too. I was just pretending."

He holds my gaze for a long moment. I think about what happened earlier, think about the lights around the kids, about my claws, and the way the fur of the costume seemed to sprout from my body. Gwen saying that I became Krampus. This is the moment that I realize I can be more than just an orphan with a terrible job and a crush on the evil daughter of my evil boss.

Briefly I worry about what this is going to do to my already almost non-existent sex life. It's only a small quibble. I look down at Gwendolyn, sleeping the sleep of evil. There must be other women like her out there, who find big hairy beasts appealing. I bet some of them aren't even evil. There's somebody for everyone. Surely Krampus is no exception.

I nod. Santa winks.

When the change happens, I grow tall. My legs lengthen and my hoof hardens and my horns reach for the sky. I know that the whisk thing I'm carrying is really a bundle of birch switches. The basket on my back is vast inside.

I'm not confused any more. I know just what to do. I lope off into the trees as the bells of Santa's sleigh jingle through the night sky overhead.

* * *

Elizabeth Twist is a speculative fiction writer living in Hamilton, Ontario. Her short fiction has appeared in Dark Faith: Invocations, Suction Cup Dreams, Enchanted Conversation, and is collected in Six by Twist, available on Amazon. She blogs about fiction and weirdness at elizabethtwist.com.

The Second Night of Krampus:

THE WICKED CHILD

by Elise Forier Edie

Inspiration: Elise used to love the Christmas season, and took great delight in its celebration of peace, love, beauty and joy. Today, she finds Christmas distasteful and upsetting, and sets her teeth every October against the seasonal onslaught of commercial exhortations to be more covetous, more ostentatious and more greedy. In the midst of such topsy-turvy values, she wondered how a truly virtuous person would react and behave. It was with this in mind that she set about writing "The Wicked Child."

The bishop and his companion had come to her grandfather's inn every autumn for as long as Tuva could remember.

It was always a great event, for the bishop rented rooms until nearly winter and paid lavish sums at a time of year when very few visitors traveled to the Arctic Circle. Everyone in the village, from the tanner's boy to the reeve, talked of his arrival, of how he would always come by reindeer sleigh, wrapped in white furs and purple velvet, how he tossed gold coins and sweets to the children, chuckling and smiling, and how his dark companion sat silent and grave by his side, a single, stick-straight shadow in the bishop's sparkling cloud of beneficence.

Once Tuva's grandmother ventured to ask what brought the bishop and his assistant so far north at such a prohibitive time of year, when the snow fell sometimes four feet in a night, trees rattled with ice crystals, and clouds blanketed the world in vast swaths of freezing fog. The bishop seemed to contemplate this question most seriously, his shrewd gaze meeting the grandmother's frank and curious one, his round face flickering in the candlelight. At last he answered gravely. "Why, I love to behold unmolested God's seasonal lightshow in the winter sky. It renews my faith and allows me to celebrate His spirit in the clearest way possible." He gestured at his companion and continued. "Is it not so for you, dear Peter?"

But the bishop's dark companion remained silent, folding lines and shadows into his gaunt cheeks as he frowned and shook his head. But Tuva saw his eyes twinkling like snowflakes in moonlight, as he glanced her way. She twinkled back at him, hoping he could see, even though she had stuffed herself into a corner of the great room, far from the fire, where she was most likely to remain unnoticed and therefore unbeaten.

Tuva was her name, but her grandfather called her "Brat" and her grandmother called her "Spawn." They hurled both these names at her, and many other worse ones, along with cuffs, kicks, and pinches, which was why Tuva preferred to hide in dark corners when she could. They had called her dead mother "The Ruination of Our Son" and the "Curse of Our Hopes." Of her father they spoke not at all.

The villagers whispered more about it, how Tuva's mother had been a beautiful gypsy queen, with clouds of black curls and lithe brown arms. The miller's daughter gushed that she had danced into the village with the Summer People, and Tuva's father, the innkeeper's only son, had taken one look at her lush lips and black eyes and fallen head over heels in love. The green grocer murmured sadly about how the innkeeper's son had followed the gypsy queen to the southern lands, where he died inconveniently and tragically (for such things happened in the south, as everyone knew). And the stable lad liked to say that when the Summer People returned to the village three years later, they brought with them a wretched story and a black-haired babe. The Summer People left Tuva at the inn, making signs of the evil eye as they fled. And everyone in the village agreed not to touch Tuva or talk to her for she was a "Danger to Their Souls" and "A Very Wicked Child."

"I tell you, I thought of dashing her brains with river rocks and leaving the Spawn in the forest to die," said Tuva's grandmother to the bishop one morning, as he dined on split peas and salty ham. "She is as bad as they come; as black haired and black eyed as the foul fiend who seduced my Yngvar, and that's the truth. But Christian charity stilled my hand and so did the sight of her face. For she has my son's face, God bless us all, right down to the bones, even as she has that harlot's blood." The grandmother ground out through her clenched teeth. "She's all I have left of him, curse her to hell, and so she lives under my roof for now."

The bishop shot a quick glance at Tuva, as she shivered behind her curtain of tangled hair. Then he said mildly to the grandmother, "Wicked children will be punished soundly, and good ones rewarded, as God judges, dear woman. Or don't they teach that in this village?"

"It's so," said the grandmother darkly. "But the child must be beaten often anyway, lest her gypsy ways lead the rest of us into ruin."

Though the bishop claimed to travel north in autumn so that he might enjoy the miraculous northern lights, Tuva never once saw him look at the sky. Instead he spent endless hours in his rooms, pouring over papers, which seemed to be nothing more than lists of names, muttering to himself and making checkmarks, his plump cheeks quivering. But his companion, whom he called Peter, often went out into the night, especially when the aurora borealis burned. Then he would stand very still in the snow, his long fingers clasped at the small of his back, hollow cheeks turned to the sky, until his black coat glistened with snow and ice.

One night he gestured at Tuva, as she crouched by the doorway of the inn, keeping her thin bare feet warm under her ragged skirt. "Come here," the bishop's companion said.

Tuva tiptoed toward him cautiously. He was so very tall and thin! And even in the light of the arcing, mysterious night rainbows, she could see how brightly his eyes burned. When she drew near enough, he suddenly snatched her up in his arms.

"It's not right that you should be so underdressed when the nights are so cold," he said gently.

Tuva said nothing at first, for her heart beat fast and her throat closed. But soon she noticed how his body gave off delicious heat; how his coat seemed to be lined with soft fur; and how good he smelled, like peat fires and pine needles and smoke. Gradually she unclenched her body and nestled into his embrace; for it was very nice to watch the sky in his arms, the stars sparkling between great silvery night flowers, which blossomed into impossible colors.

Tuva did not know how long he held her but finally he asked, his voice seeming to rumble through her whole body, "Are you really as wicked as your grandmother says?"

Tuva had been sucking her thumb and nodding into sleep, but she answered automatically, "I am the worst of children and I am cursed to hell for all eternity, sir."

"I thought so," said Peter. He sounded pleased.

The bishop and Peter left, as they always did, on the first of December, taking their baggage and lists and ink stands with them. Tuva never saw them depart. Instead, they seemed to vanish in an instant, like a pair of candle flames snuffed by the wind. Then there would be the long, dark winter, with only school and church and the occasional group of reindeer herders to break the cold monotony, until spring returned with her green leaves and other wonders.

"St. Nicholas brought me candies," a flaxen haired girl announced at school, not long after the bishop and his companion had departed.

All the children at Tuva's school were flaxen haired and looked like the plump angels in picture books, with fat cheeks and rosy complexions. Their parents had warned them not to touch the gypsy's child, but they would have despised Tuva anyway, for she was thin and dark and quick, and did sums better than anyone. They pinched her often and called her "Bohunk" and "Ink Face" and said she did sums well because she was a born cheater, a "gyp." Tuva knew better than to talk to them, but she listened avidly as they compared notes about St. Nicholas. All over the schoolyard, the good saint was found wanting.

"He brought me only one toy soldier!"

"I wanted lemon sours, not peppermints."

"I only got an orange."

"What did you get?"

On and on they grumbled and compared, ignoring the last precious slivers of noonday sun.

"But one chocolate!"

"And my sister got a sled."

"I wanted so much more."

Of course, Tuva had got no chocolates, or peppermints or oranges from St. Nicholas. Tuva never got a single gift at all, for Tuva was a wicked child. All she ever received was an enormous bundle of sticks or a bulging sack full of coal from St. Nicholas's helper, the devil Krampus. "And a fitting gift for the likes of you, Spawn," her grandmother was fond of saying.

But what Tuva never told anyone, least of all her grandmother, and certainly never the ungrateful cherubs at school, was that she liked the coal and sticks very much, more than she would have liked candied dolls. For every Krampus-night was the warmest night of the year for Tuva—who was hardly ever warm in winter—and as she heaped her precious fuel on the fire, and watched the coals glow orange and red, she thanked the evil Krampus again and again in her mind and hoped that he could hear her.

One year, the same year that she had watched the Northern Lights with Peter, Krampus brought the usual bundle of switches for Tuva, but nestled in the middle, smooth and golden, was a special stick, with tiny holes poked in the sides. Tuva had seen pictures of pipers in her schoolbooks and knew the golden stick could make music, if properly used. So she set it aside in the mess of rags she used as a bed. Then she burned the rest of her present with her dark brows drawn together in a thoughtful frown.

Good children she knew played the spinet and the harp, while grown-ups sat stiffly in straight-backed chairs and drowsed or clapped politely. But a piper played the devil's music, and sometimes the music of war. And these sounds stirred the blood, giving rise to improper thoughts and wild urges. Tuva wondered at the golden pipe, and what Krampus had meant by giving it to her. Did he know it was in the bundle? Had it been a mistake? Should she learn to play it, or burn it with the rest of the switches? Tuva didn't want to make Krampus angry. He was, after all, the only being in the world who ever shown her any kindness.

All night long, and for many days afterwards, while the good children at school fretted over how St. Nicholas had cheated them, Tuva wrestled with whether or not to destroy to the pipe. At last, just after midwinter's day, when the sun glimmered on the horizon for a frozen breath longer than it had the day before, Tuva decided to keep it and teach herself to play. She began slipping into the barn every night to practice, after her grandparents, and indeed all the village, had taken to their beds.

The music came quickly, much to the delight of the cow, the cat, the donkey and the ducks, who slept in the barn all winter. Tuva's secret pipings first sounded like birds cheeping, then dogs howling, then like a proper gypsy's tune, whistling the earth spirits up from their winter slumber. By spring Tuva could play sweet songs to the new kittens, ducklings and calves. And all summer her grandfather remarked at how peaceful and blessed the inn seemed to be—how fruitful the garden, how satisfied the guests, how happy every creature in the pasture.

"Thank God your wicked nature has failed to infect my beasts and garden," he spat to Tuva, as he cuffed her.

"God has blessed us for our charity," the grandmother fluted, as she planted a kick on Tuva's shin. "Although he could bless us more, if I do say so myself. The duck has raised but three ducklings, we have had but four hay cuttings this year and the neighbor's cow gives more milk than ours, though the cream is not as sweet."

When the bishop and Peter returned in the fall to rent their rooms as always, Tuva had danced and blown in her pipes all year long. The bishop looked at her coolly from under his thick white eyebrows. But Peter patted her dark head, not seeming to mind the dirt and straw snarled in her curls.

"How is the wicked child?" the bishop inquired politely of the grandmother, still looking Tuva up and down.

"As disgusting as ever," the grandmother replied. "She spends all her time in the barn with the animals, more animal herself, if you ask me."

"Well, it seems to agree with her," said the bishop. He raised a silver eyebrow at Peter.

"Yes, she's taller," said Peter. "And there's a bloom to her cheeks."

"More's the pity," the grandmother intoned. "To have a healthy grandchild should be a blessing, but of course I was cursed with a gypsy's child so it matters not to me."

"Yes, I can see that," said the bishop dryly.

As with all the years before, the bishop and Peter closeted themselves in their rooms with stacks of candles and lists of names, muttering endlessly in the flickering light, while it grew steadily darker and colder outside. Tuva wondered if she would see Peter in the snow again—she had very fond memories of his warm, furry coat, and the dancing display of color in the sky. But every time she ventured into the cold to peer wonderingly at the Northern Lights, she did it alone. For Peter stayed inside with the bishop that season, working both day and night.

By late November, the kittens had grown into cats, and were making themselves fat on mice and cream; the little calf had muscled into half a cow and the ducklings had transformed into a squabbling flock. Tuva sat in the barn in the dark, as was her custom now, playing her pipes to the animals, while one day turned into the next, and church bells chimed the midnight hour. She played a tune of her own making, weaving her feelings in and out of the things she had seen. She piped about the sparkling snow on the branches of fir trees, about the cold moon shining blue and silver on the inn's roof, about the villagers, dressed in their finery, comparing themselves to one another in church. Her song held the croak of ebony feathered ravens, the wild, sweet tang of winterberries, the sadness of the snow-covered cemetery and the joy of sunlight's radiant fingers, reaching from the horizon. When she finished, there was only the sound of cats purring from the straw, and so it startled her terribly when Peter spoke from the darkness. Where had he come from?

"You have someone to teach you to play the pipes, child?" Peter asked.

"No," said Tuva. "I taught myself, sir."

"Your music makes me want to dance and shout and be a better man."

"That's too bad." She sighed. "For everyone knows proper music makes people fall asleep in their chairs." Peter laughed as Tuva added, "It's because I'm so wicked, I expect. The only music I can make would be the devil's music."

"Although the animals seem at peace," Peter remarked.

"Well, Grandmother says animals have no souls."

"What do you think?"

Tuva winced at her own wickedness but answered truthfully. "I'm not sure she's right about that."

"Well. You are indeed as terrible as they say," Peter said with a laugh. He added, "Please play some more on your pipes, won't you?"

So Tuva did, far into the cold winter night, hoping by doing so she did not damn poor Peter's soul to hell.

Again, as before, the bishop and Peter departed just before Krampus night. And just as always Tuva received a bundle of sticks and coal, which she burned with great delight and gratitude. And nestled in the middle of her sticks were two more wooden flutes of different sizes. The large one sounded to her like the thrum of the ocean, echoing in secret caves full of gold and shipwrecked jewels. The tiny flute sounded like clouds of butterflies, chasing dust motes in an orchard of fragrant orange blossoms.

That winter, while Tuva played at night, she also stamped her feet and danced in the straw, for she found it warmed her very nicely. The cows and the donkey helped with the stamping, and the cats and ducks added their exclamations, and the resulting noise was so mighty, it was a miracle Tuva did not wake the whole village, let alone her grandparents, sleeping in the inn next door. But she never did wake a single soul. Instead, everyone in town whispered of the wondrous dreams they had, all that winter long.

"I dreamed of a dark girl, with perfumed oil on her hands, who stroked me in a tent in Araby, until my skin glowed, while the sand outside scoured the whole world with gold dust," whispered the baker's wife to her sister. "I have such a longing in my heart now, for the sun, and for that maid's hands. No one ever touched me with such love, not once in my life."

"I dreamed I sang my soul out in a concert hall," wept the preacher to his wife. "And my soul transfixed the angels with its beauty while all the world held its breath. And now I know I have wasted my life, for I never sang with such feeling, not once, only talked and talked, inspiring no one, not even myself."

"I dreamed of my dead brother George," cried Tuva's grandmother, when only the cats could hear her. "And he said to me, 'Maya! Will you go to your grave having never laughed like I did?' For George could laugh so hard he cried. And everyone around laughed with him. And I see now, I never truly enjoy anything since he died. And I don't know that I know how anymore."

And so it went, throughout the village, dreams upon dreams every night all winter, while Tuva's secret, midnight music blew from house to house on the icy air. And every dark morning the villagers awakened with their wishes streaming down their cheeks, and their throats stopped cold with unspoken feelings.

One day the butcher, who had dreamed the same dream for a fortnight, of kissing the tailor's daughter until she swooned, grabbed the poor girl in church, and nearly suffocated her, planting kiss after kiss on her lips and her neck, weeping with lust and embarrassment.

"I dreamed of you. I dreamed of you." He wept, as they pried him from her arms. "I dreamed of you and the dream said that you would love me back."

"I do love you," cried the tailor's daughter, when his lips had finally left her own. "But I have been promised to another. So we can only love in our dreams."

"Then the dream is a curse," growled the butcher.

"A curse!" the echo reverberated throughout the village. "A dream!" "A dream!" "A curse!"

And with that, the villagers took up their torches and went to the inn, for who else would make a curse but Tuva, as black in her soul as her wanton mother? And naturally, when they searched Tuva's rags and her pitiful, filthy bed, they found the pipes, and beat her with them, and then threw them on the fire.

What followed were a hard spring and summer, for Tuva's grandparents banished her from the inn, and the village citizens stoned her on sight. She had to run away to the woods, or risk being burned for a witch. Luckily, the animals took pity on her. The barn cats brought her fish, and the ducks laid their eggs where she could find them, and the donkey helped her gather firewood to stay warm on cold nights. She bathed in the river and found an abandoned shepherd's hut to sleep in. She tried to carve a flute, but had no luck with it. So she stole some torn hides from the tanner's refuse bin, and stitched herself a drum.

By fall, Tuva was brown as a sapling and as supple, thin, strong and hard. Her wild black hair cascaded down her back, washed clean and shining from river water. Her dark eyes glistened with fury, as she overheard the village children on the forest path, lamenting their lot in life, how they were never allowed as many sweets as they wanted, and how tired they were of parties and larks. She beat her drum savagely, though it was the fat children she wanted to beat; and she burned small twigs and fir boughs, though she longed to burn down the village; and she sang her songs to the forest creatures, though she wished she could sing of her pain and hate to the people who had shunned her, perhaps driving them all mad once and for all, so they would eat one another and die in blood and horror. Tuva knew her thoughts were sinful, but she could not seem to stop herself from thinking them. Still she stopped her hands from wreaking the havoc they longed to do.

One day, just as the fist of night was tightening fully on the autumn days, a visitor came to Tuva's hut. It was Peter, the bishop's dark companion. "I heard the Very Wicked Child was living alone in the woods, having charmed the whole village with her music."

"I did not mean to charm them," Tuva said. "I was just playing what I knew."

"Well. You have a gift," said Peter. "So you couldn't help it." And he smiled while she scowled.

Tuva said, "My music made the villagers unhappy. It is because I am so bad that they were hurt by it."

Peter touched her hair. It was clean now that she had left her grandmother's care, and it fell in a rippling waterfall of shining darkness from her smooth, clear brow. "Foolish people never want to be reminded of how great they can be," he said. "But that doesn't mean they shouldn't have been reminded, Tuva. You did the villagers a great favor, although they were too stupid to see it. And you gave them something wonderful; you gave them a dream." He smiled. "And I am here to do you a favor, my wicked, wicked child."

"What can that be?" Tuva asked.

"I am here to take you to where you belong."

And then Peter did a very strange thing, so strange that the cats sat up and blinked their jewel-like eyes, and Tuva fell down hard in the snow. For he took off his cloak and his shoes and his hat, and indeed every stitch of his clothing. And Tuva saw that his skin was covered with fur and that golden horns sprouted from the top of his head and she gave a little cry, that was half a sob and half of something more.

"You are my Krampus!" she exclaimed. And then, "Are you here to take me to hell?"

"You are indeed too wicked for this place. So I am taking you to a place I expect your villagers would think most hellish."

"Ah," said Tuva with a laugh. "Then I expect I shall like it very much." And with that, she jumped into his warm, strong arms, and planted a kiss on his hideous face.

And for years afterwards, the villagers spoke of Tuva in fearful voices and the stories about her grew more and more outlandish. They said she had been a powerful witch, who changed into a cat in the night. They said she had seduced all the men and women in the village with music, though she was only a child. They said her evil was so great, the devil himself had taken her in his arms, and now she sat on his right hand and ruled with her mother in hell. And they fretted and fumed and dozed and ate too much, and felt only alive when they gossiped.

But Krampus had merely taken Tuva to the Southern Lands, where a turquoise sea caressed a golden beach, and a warm sun laughed itself into sparkles on the waves, and whole tribes of people ran naked on the sand. And there Tuva was welcomed with open arms and she played pipes to her heart's content, for these people loved music and dreaming and dancing almost as much as they loved laughter and games. There was no St. Nicholas's night in this place, for the people here gave gifts hourly to one another, instead of waiting for once a year; and so they wanted for nothing, and never piled their hopes and wishes on just one day. Instead, a steady stream of love and laughter washed into Tuva's life, where once there had only been sorrow and pain.

The only thing she missed about her old life were her animals, and so she asked Krampus if they might be allowed to join her, for he visited her quite often. He brought them to her the following year. The ducks took to the warm water quite happily, the cows and the donkey accepted their new lot with the same peace they accepted everything, and the cats enjoyed themselves thoroughly, snaking in between rocks and lazing in the sun.

Once Tuva asked Krampus how it was that the people in the north had gotten things mixed up in their minds, so that they thought enjoyment a sin, acceptance an evil, and a gift something to be measured against another's good fortune. Krampus shrugged and said he didn't know, only that every year he and the Bishop of Myra went up to those cold and fretful lands, and tried to teach the people about joy. So far it had been to no avail.

"Why most of them can't even see a true gift for what it is," he sighed, while Tuva ran her hands through his fur (she did so love to touch his fur). "A despairing old couple receives the gift of their only grandchild, and reviles it. A community bereft of inspiration is given the gift of dreaming, and throws it away in the forest like trash. They label things 'good' and 'bad' and 'good enough' and 'not enough,' while never seeing anything for what it truly is. For if truth and beauty and love of life must be labeled wickedness, then heaven loves a wicked child, my Tuva. And so do I."

At that, Tuva laughed and kissed his cheek. Then she played her pipes and they danced the night away.

* * *

Elise Forier Edie is a professional author and playwright, based in southern California. Her most recent work of fiction, a paranormal romance novella, entitled *The Devil in Midwinter,* was released this year by World Weaver Press.

The Third Night of Krampus:

MARCHING KRAMPUS

by Jill Corddry

Inspiration: "Marching Krampus" was inspired by an old photograph Jill stumbled across in one of the many internet lists posted on social media sites. A few weeks went by and she couldn't shake that particular image, so after many starts and stops, the tale of a naughty little boy and his sister emerged.

Christmas came and went with little fanfare, outside the usual chaos of the Hauer household. Felix was relieved when nothing out of the ordinary happened. It wasn't like Felix didn't try to behave, but with a sister like Petra, whose bobbing blonde curls simply begged to be tugged, being good was hard. Still, his stocking had been full of candies and fruits, and the wrapped presents from Saint Nicholas had been stacked high under the Christmas tree. That was the one aspect he'd been most afraid of—knowing the little pest had written to Saint Nicholas tattling on him. He knew because she'd dictated the letter out loud as her large, childish print filled the blank paper. Given the pile of presents he'd gotten, Saint Nicholas didn't get the note. Or didn't care. Probably understood that boys will be boys. And curls occasionally need to be pulled.

By the time February rolled around, he'd grown tired of the now mostly broken toys and presents he'd received. So Felix turned his attention to Petra's pile of goody-two-shoes earned loot. Especially that blasted doll with the real corn silk hair. So like her own. She carried it everywhere, treating the stupid thing like it was a real baby. Any time Mother asked her to put it down, Petra carried on and on, the tears welling, magnifying her already giant blue eyes, until it was easier to let her hold the stupid thing during dinner. Or take it to school. Or anywhere and everywhere she went.

Until one March day she didn't.

It sat at the tiny table that hosted Petra's endless tea parties, alongside a one-eyed teddy bear, assorted worn stuffed animals, and an empty chair. Felix crept into her room, expecting her to hiss and jump out at him. But the pest was nowhere to be seen. He ran gentle fingers along the soft hair of the doll. Without conscious planning, he snatched the doll from its pink-and-white flowered seat and dashed to his room, shoving the thing under his bed, behind the piles of clothes and toys.

Petra's howling scream five minutes later was so loud and long, the neighbors came running, concerned over some imagined emergency. You'd think they'd be used to Petra by now.

Mother was at his door as soon as she sent the neighbors away. She didn't need to say anything; the crossed arms and pinched line between her eyes were as familiar to him as his own blonde hair and blue eyes.

"Felix!" she snapped, her tone weary. "Just give it back to your sister."

He pondered what might happen if he 'fessed up now. Might get a spanking, but he was used to the feel of Mother's wooden spoon on his backside. And it probably wasn't a crime worthy of Father's leather belt. Probably wouldn't get dessert tonight, but he could always sneak down to the kitchen after everyone was sound asleep and help himself. Not that he wouldn't do that tonight anyways.

So no dessert was the worst of it. And he didn't want to give up his prize for something he was going to take later anyway. He shook his head in what he hoped was convincing confusion. "Give what back?"

"My baby," Petra screeched, flinging herself onto his bed and taking a swing at his nose with her tiny fist. Not that Mother's selective sight would notice that.

His sister's face was a splotchy mess of snot and tears as she continued to sob and simultaneously strike him.

"Don't know whatcher talking about," he said. "Just been sitting here with my comics." He gestured at the pile of brightly colored books now strewn about the floor. Thanks to Petra the pest. But he'd have to clean them up.

Petra turned pleading eyes to Mother. "Make him give my baby back," she cried.

"Don't have it," he protested again, scowling this time. "Just 'cuz she lost it, don't go blaming me."

Mother gathered Petra in a hug and murmured, "Let's go look in your room, darling. I'm sure you just put her down somewhere."

As they left his room, Petra clinging to their mother, protesting the whole time, he grinned at her and ran his finger across his throat.

Now, what to do to the blasted thing . . .

A few days later, the brilliant idea came to Felix as he doodled on his desk during math class. The rest of the day passed with increasing slowness, until the bell finally rang. He ran home, knowing Mother and Petra would be shopping for at least an hour.

As Felix gathered the supplies he'd need, a few chuckles escaped his lips. He knew, even though he was only ten years old, that an opportunity equal to this would never again present itself, so he worked carefully on the once-in-a-lifetime gift.

The car pulled into the driveway before he could believe it. It would take them a few minutes to gather the groceries, but that time would pass all too quickly. He dashed to Petra's room and placed her precious baby exactly where he'd stolen it, at the small tea time table.

Mother's chatter wafted through the door as she and Petra came inside. He heard the crinkle of bags as Mother sorted the groceries.

Heard his sister "helping." And finally heard her little feet running down the hallway.

That scream again. At least the neighbors stayed home this time.

She ran into his room, clutching the now mostly-bald baby doll to her chest. "I'm gonna tell Saint Nicholas!" she sobbed and slammed his door.

* * *

Petra insisted on hauling that stupid, scalped baby around with her. She glared at Felix every time she ran a loving hand along the spiky hairdo. With a sigh, Mother placed dinner on the table. As always, no one had been able to convince the pest to leave her toys in her room.

The door creaked open. They all turned their heads in unison, Father with a fork partially in his mouth. Two devils filled the space. They were almost men, being nearly the same height and shape of men, wearing men's clothing. They could almost be men. Except for their faces. Those dark, horrible faces. Oddly angled horns stood out from the crowns of their heads; one had a long, shiny goatee-like thing hanging from its chin.

The monsters came up behind Felix silently; his family did nothing but stare, their eyes wide with fear.

One of them pulled Felix from his chair, and still no one protested. It wrapped an arm around his chest and backed toward the door they'd both come in. Felix's arms and legs felt heavy, but he offered no resistance. Couldn't. Even as it felt like they were picking through his mind.

With a sudden flick of a wrist, the monster not holding him flipped open a straight razor. Felix felt cold metal press against his scalp as the blade slithered from side to side. Pale hair fell like straw, clinging to his dark jacket and shorts, covering his shoes. It was over in seconds.

Felix stood as the monster carefully tucked the blade inside its jacket. They departed as silently as they'd come.

"Krampus," Petra whispered. She glared at her brother. "Told you I was gonna tell Saint Nicholas."

* * *

Jill Corddry started telling stories at an early age and hasn't stopped since. These days, Jill writes in between taking care of twin toddlers and soaking up the California sunshine. Her stories are published in *Lakeside Circus, Bewildering Stories*, and in the James Ward Kirk anthology *Demonic Possession*. She is a member of the PNWA and the California Writers Club.

The Fourth Night of Krampus:

PEPPERMINT STICKS
by Colleen H. Robbins

Inspiration: Colleen writes, "My grandfather's tales of Santa's evil brother Krampus made him sound like a goblin, yet Santa not only works with elves, but is said to be one. I just had to explore the dichotomy between them."

Late December

Faint with cold and hunger, tired of job-hunting in this impossible economy, and kicking himself for indulging in an elaborate tattoo—a decision that had bitten him in the ass when he applied to the military—Steven clutched his threadbare coat closed and stumbled into the employment office. No glitz and glamour here, but no death or prison, either. Just a grimy sort of hope.

"Good morning, Steven." Young, petite, and perky, the only meals his counselor Pamela missed were side effects of her anorexia.

"I'm afraid I don't have any interviews lined up for you today." The skinny old European Santa decorating her desk teetered precariously when her oversized sleeve brushed it. "I do have a survey. It's a one-shot, but the client pays two hundred dollars for it." She handed him a faded envelope.

He opened it carefully. A paper cut would really help his cold-numbed fingers. Right. Inside the envelope lay a sheet of cream colored, crisply folded paper. It crackled when he unfolded it, giving off a scent that reminded him of his grandmother's cinnamon rolls.

A single question took up the entire page in hand-drawn calligraphy:

"What is a Fey? Please illustrate your answer."

Funny, Steven thought. He actually knew the answer to that. Who would have thought that Shakespeare would help him get a job? He quickly sketched out some scenes from *A Midsummer Night's Dream* that included Titania, Oberon, and Puck.

"Wait a minute while I fax this to the client, and then I'll pay you for your efforts." Pamela's heels clacked across the room.

He listened to the squeal of the fax machine, the general chatter in the room between other clients and their counselors, and the jarring ring of the telephone followed by transfer noises around the room. A moment later his counselor came back looking more puzzled than perky. "Mr. Krampus wants to speak with you to set up an interview." She punched the blinking button on her phone.

Steven took the receiver. "Hello?"

The voice was surprisingly deep, the clipped words rushing across the phone lines. "B. Peter Krampus, here. I'd like to meet with you. Do you know the Starbucks on Center Street? I'll meet you there in thirty minutes."

"Um, oka—" The phone clicked before he finished the word.

* * *

The Coffee Shop

It wasn't a Starbucks anymore, but the place still served coffee. Coffee strong enough that Steven could smell it half a block before he reached the shop. His mouth watered; his stomach clenched with hunger. The check in his pocket wouldn't help until he cashed it later, and he didn't have any cash.

The girl at the counter looked tired; a few retirees argued about politics at a corner table, nursing their morning coffees. A tall man in a suit sat in a vinyl booth behind the door.

"Mr. Krampus?"

"Steven? Come, have a seat." The voice was unmistakable. Krampus gestured at the other side of the booth. Steven slid in as Krampus opened the second of two large coffees and took a long sip.

Steven looked closely at his potential employer. A tall man, perhaps 35, but with a few fine lines around the eyes, the man's hawk nose and thin frame resembled a younger version of his job counselor's Christmas decoration, except for the peculiar twist to the ears that made them seem almost pointed. Krampus' hair swept up into an old fashioned pompadour, and Steven saw the glint of something off-white hidden within the sculpted pile. A small goatee decorated the man's chin, not quite touching his red power tie. The suit beneath looked expensive.

Krampus snapped open a folder. "Very clever drawings. I'll take you on temporarily. The job involves some travel and outdoor work, some charity—you don't mind giving out some candy at Halloween and Christmas, do you?—and a salary of $130,000 a year, payable weekly. Training is on the job." He snapped the folder shut. "Go pack your warmest clothes and I'll pick you up here tomorrow."

"I have everything I own right here, sir." Steven waited for the job offer to disappear.

The deep voice softened momentarily. "We'll stop and get you a warmer coat on the way to the hotel." Krampus finished his coffee, then dashed to the counter to order another. "Come, come."

Stomach growling loud enough to make him wince, Steven followed.

* * *

Early February

Steven, crouched in a thick, knee-length fleece-lined coat, set to an impossible task: watching the grass grow through the snow. Boring, but it paid well. The past two days had yielded no results; he expected the same of today's efforts. He sighed and refocused his eyes. A bit of green poked through the snow. Three more tendrils joined it by evening. On the fourth day, a tiny flower bud appeared. On the fifth, it appeared the same. He closed his eyes for a moment, and opened them again just in time to see a small white flower open. A drop of water clung to it, then rolled slowly upward across the petal.

Upward? He blinked twice and leaned closer. A tiny fairy, barely a quarter of an inch long and looking more like a cherub with withered wings than a proper Tinkerbell, crawled to the highest point on the flower and clung there. Breathing heavily—or as heavily as a quarter-inch long creature can—it slowly unfurled its wings. Each breath pumped fluids into the wings, stretching them larger, while simultaneously slimming the fairy. When the wings had stretched to a half an inch tall, the fairy held them in the breeze, drying them. A few breaths of wind, and the fairy fanned them experimentally: a slow flap like a condor in flight, a few moderate flaps like a bluebird in spring, the fast flap of a hummingbird. The fairy rose into the sky. Steven saw Krampus trudging through the snow beneath.

"What have you learned?" Mr. Krampus brushed Steven's left shoulder.

"Fairies are real." Steven whispered.

"You'll make a fine apprentice. Your temporary job just became permanent."

* * *

May Day

Steven crept along the muddy ground, pushing aside stick-like brush to hide beneath triplets of leaves. His face itched with tension.

The fairies avoided his hiding place, clustering around the weeping willow trees in the soggy end of Marshland Park. Teams of fairies lifted fronds and circled the trees in both directions, darting back and forth and weaving the ribbon-like branches tightly together. Almost two feet tall now, their four-part dragonfly wings buzzed. They swarmed like the rows of toy store Barbies that his sisters would never get for Christmas. Barbies and Kens, he corrected himself. The fairies had clear sexes now. The males wore loincloths of ragged leaves, while the females fashioned dresses. They resembled Tinkerbell after all.

* * *

Midsummer Night's Eve, the Summer Solstice

His leg cramping for the seventh time since he concealed himself at noon under the brush at the edge of the forest, Steven sought to will the muscles to relax. Mr. K left early, leaving Steven to observe on his own. The heady scent of meadow flowers tempted him to sleep. His cramping leg prevented it.

As sundown approached, the fairies trooped out of the forest and milled about near the rings of mushrooms and toadstools that edged the meadow. A few drifted towards the flowers, sniffing and sipping at the nectar. A few more joined them. With a rush, the entire group flew to the flowers, sniffing, sipping, and even rolling in the blossoms. It had all the trappings of a frat party of four year olds, a complete drunken mixer sprinkled with brawls.

Older, taller fey stalked past Steven, almost startling him into motion. Many resembled Mr. K: tall, thin, hawk-nosed, and with a similar ear twist. These, however, wore weapons and armor that left their wings unencumbered.

The human-sized fey waded into the fray, pulling drunken combatants out two and three at a time. Forcibly armored and handed thin swords—knives really—that gleamed silver in the moonlit darkness, the drunken fairies found themselves tossed into the mushroom rings. The battles began. Swords flashed, blood flowed, and the contests continued until a clear winner stood and cut off the wings of the loser. Winners pinned their trophy wings to the nearer trees with thorns; tall fey dragged the losers from the rings and drove them into the darkness of the forest.

One collapsed near Steven's hiding place, bleeding from dozens of slashes. The creature sobbed and moaned, reaching back to finger the stumps of its wings and grunting. It looked back at the continuing combat and gave a long hiss through needle-sharp teeth before crawling off.

Steven shuddered.

* * *

All Hallow's Eve

Steven peered out from the carefully manicured bushes at the excited mob of children, then did a double-take as Mr. K's words sunk in. "Are you for real? You want me to shoot goblins? On Halloween?" His voice rose with each phrase.

Krampus nodded. "Don't be so dramatic over a few tranquilizers."

Steven surveyed the crowded street. Throngs of little monsters ran between houses, the cries of "Trick or Treat!" rising into the twilight. "I'm not shooting kids." If he'd wanted to shoot kids, he could have just joined a gang back in the old neighborhood . . .

"Goblins have cat-eyes."

After watching the increasingly hyperactive children for over an hour, Steven noticed a few sluggish children with a fistful of candy wrappers. He pointed at two of them standing together. "Are they . . ." He trailed off, searching from side to side. No coffee smell. No Mr. K. When did the man leave?

Steven snorted. Mr. K would probably return with a grande latte from the local coffee shop. He had never seen anyone drink so much coffee.

A sluggish child stumbled nearby, crashing through the bushes and almost landing in Steven's arms. Up close, Steven could see the slight fold inside the child's ear, similar to Mr. K's. The child opened a glassy eye, the cat-like pupil contracting. A goblin!

He searched one-handed through his ammunition pouch, slowly pulled out a tranquilizer dart and flipped the cap off before slipping the point into the goblin's back. The goblin gasped and collapsed to the ground, unconscious. Unsure what to do, Steven stayed in the bushes, cradling the goblin until he remembered the plastic zip ties Mr. K had given him.

The sun vanished beneath the horizon, leaving blood red clouds to slowly fade. A car drove up directly in front of the bushes and popped the trunk.

The window rolled down, revealing Mr. Krampus. "Put him inside."

"Is it safe to lift him?" Steven remembered the teeth.

"Did he pass out from candy? Did you tranquilize him? He's safe."

Steven stuffed the goblin into the trunk, rearranging the other four chest-high bodies—two of them with normal human ears—before he could close it. Glancing around to make certain no one had seen him, he slipped into the passenger seat and slid down as far as he could.

* * *

November 2nd

The wind whistled through the slat walls of the cabin. Steven tied the last knot as the goblin shivered its way back to consciousness. Over the last day and a half, the two normal children had developed a twisted fold in their ears, a fold that had not been there before. All three true goblins slouched, held mostly upright by the ropes that tied their chests, arms, and ankles to the chairs. Their costumes still lay in puddles of bright fabric on the floor.

While waiting for Mr. Krampus to return from Caribou Coffee, Steven examined his charges. Scars marred the true goblins' skins, slashes long healed and some more recently acquired. Two mounds of knotted scar tissue darkened the skin between their shoulder blades. The two changing children had similar scars, scars left during their punishment the day before.

Steven shuddered, remembering the venom in Mr. K's voice.

"Naughty, naughty," followed by the crack of a whip. The strikes left bloody gashes, and Mr. K's deep chuckle nearly drowned out the children's screams and whimpers.

He shuddered again. The goblins glared at him and snarled.

What did Mr. K want with these twisted children, anyway? Why punish them?

The door banged. The goblins and transforming children struggled in their chairs, snapping with long fairy teeth at the ropes that bound them.

Mr. K threw a bag of lollipops to Steven. "Feed them candy. Have you learned nothing?"

Steven tore the bag open and unwrapped a lollipop. Five goblin heads turned simultaneously, noses wrinkling and eyes tracking the piece of candy. Steven held the lollipop at arm's length towards the first goblin, edging closer an inch at a time.

In a flash, the goblin extended its neck like a Jack-in-the-box and snapped the candy from his fingers, leaving a bare half-inch of rolled paper stick behind. Crunching followed.

Steven eyed his fingers, silently counting them while he took a deep breath to calm his racing heart. He glanced at Mr. K expecting to see amusement, but the man simply watched, one eyebrow slightly raised.

"You could have warned me."

"Be careful of their teeth."

Frowning, he looked back at the goblin. The creature ceased crunching. The stick fell from the corner of its mouth, followed by a line of glittering drool.

Something didn't feel right, he thought. He grew more uncomfortable as he fed lollipops to the other four with the same results.

Mr. Krampus retied the goblins' arms and legs. "They're almost ready. Bring the van around, Steven. We're going to the airport."

* * *

November 4th

The Cessna landed on the snow-glazed field. A dozen chest-high elves dressed in red and green drove a sleigh out—a real sleigh, with skis on the bottom and a horse in front—and loaded the bound goblins in the back. They drove off toward a large warehouse that seemed to double as a hangar. Mr. Krampus taxied the Cessna inside, then took a handful of candy sticks from a bag stowed beneath the front seat.

Steven smelled peppermint. "Not again."

"I'll distribute them this time." Mr. K walked across the warehouse. He held the peppermint sticks up with a gloved hand. The elves came running, clustering around until each held a stick. They drifted away, faces vacant, sucking on their candy.

In the next room, while all five goblins struggled in their ropes, Mr. K tossed a bag of peppermint sticks to Steven, then stalked across the room and wrapped his arms around an obese man in paint-stained gray sweats.

"We meet again, brother."

"Peter! I'm so glad to see you again." The brother's voice shook with suppressed laughter.

"Always a pleasure, Nick."

"I have another naughty list for you. Don't forget it when you leave."

Steven was surprised how much the two resembled each other, down to the hawk nose and ear twist, though Nick's white hair and beard stuck out at all angles. So different from Mr. K's sculpted pompadour and carefully trimmed goatee.

Steven opened the bag and pushed peppermint sticks into the goblins' snapping jaws. Their faces glowed. It became Steven's job to feed the goblins peppermint sticks after preparing coffee for Mr. K and his brother each morning. He just hoped Mr. K wouldn't ask him to help punish the children who had not yet completed the transformation.

The next day, two of the goblins begged for peppermint before Steven had even unwrapped the candy. Elves swarmed in and took them away.

The following day another goblin begged, also to be taken away.

A planeload of goblins arrived in the afternoon, twenty chest-high creatures that the elves quickly strapped into chairs next to his remaining charges. Steven groaned and unwrapped more peppermint sticks.

He felt dirtier and dirtier. Each day about half the remaining group—and the two planeloads that arrived in succession over the next week—begged for the sticks. The elves ran in and removed the begging goblins. Steven dreamt about the old neighborhood. He could have stayed there, working security for the pimps who rewarded their girls with heroin. But no, he fought and clawed his way out of the slums, attending and failing out of college, scraping for a job that would let him stay away from the grime. He couldn't believe he'd walked into the same job, this time addicting children. Fey children, and children who became fey, but still children. How could Mr. K do it?

When they returned to the city two weeks later, he found himself disgusted with the penthouse apartment he shared with Mr. Krampus. He tossed and turned half the night, and finally stumbled into the bathroom half-asleep during the man's shower. Steven stopped dead at the profile seen through the patterned glass door: the short stubs of cut wings.

He shuffled through the kitchen making Mr. K's morning coffee.

"What's this morning's flavor?"

"Hazelnut."

Mr. Krampus slowly drank it, savoring his coffee as he had every day for most of a year.

Steven left a little earlier than usual to do his afternoon errands. He stopped by the bank and closed his account. He visited other banks around town, banks that had branches across the nation, and opened smaller accounts. That done, he stopped to pick up coffee, cream, and a few other odds and ends on his way back.

The next morning, he stirred the coffee carefully.

Mr. K called out from the next room, "What flavor are you making today?"

"A version of Irish coffee."

"I like whiskey. It's sweet."

"I'm adding something a little different." Steven opened the airplane sized bottle of Rumplemintz Peppermint Schnapps and poured it in. He stowed the other three small bottles in the back of a cabinet behind some dusty cans of soup. He wondered how many it would take . . .

* * *

Colleen H. Robbins has been writing since she was nine years old. If she doesn't write often enough she gets distracted and hits her head on the side of the pool while swimming backstroke. She's currently writing a YA fantasy novel series that involves problems teenagers face today.

The Fifth Night of Krampus:

RING, LITTLE BELL, RING

by Caren Gussoff

Inspiration: Caren says, "Our December holidays happen during the darkest, coldest part of the year, and, to me, have always suggested a sinister presence lurking beneath the façade of "Jolly Old Saint Nick." I fell in love with the idea of Krampusnacht because it acknowledges that underlying menace that we here in the modern West try to ignore. "Ring, Little Bell" grew from a demented extrapolation about the spouse of Krampus; Santa has a partner, so it seemed natural that his shadowy partner should have one too . . . and, of course, in order to marry, one must date."

The man I love is singing a Christmas carol.

Kling, Glöckchen . . .

He has a lovely singing voice. An edged tenor. It suits his face, his body: vertical, long, elegant, and a little cold.

klingelingeling!

When I first met this man I love, I searched his face and body for traces of anyone I had ever known before. I never found any. He was new. A complete stranger; I found that very attractive.

Kling, Glöckchen, kling!

I know the song now, though he has slowed the tempo, and is singing in German. "Ring, Little Bell, Ring."

Laßt mich ein, ihr Kinder!

Children, let me enter.

Ist so kalt der Winter!
The winter is so cold.
Öffnet mir die Türen!
Open me your doorway.
Laßt mich nicht erfrieren!
Not to freeze this day.
Kling . . .
Before tonight, I didn't know he could sing. Or that he knew much German. Or the other thing.
Glöckchen . . .
I pull my legs up so I can bury my face in my knees. I close my eyes and try not to breathe.
klingelingeling!
So I can hear him better.
Kling, Glöckchen . . .
So that I can stay really quiet.
kling!
So that I can fully fit behind the pantry shelf.
Kling, Glöckchen, kling!
So that he won't find me.
Klingelingeling!

* * *

Drew Case tripped and fell out of a tenth story window. A simple, terrible accident.

Drew and I had worked together closely. A cohort of two, we studied deviance in a sociology department known for labor policy and political economy analysis.

I liked Drew. He would have liked for me to love him. I didn't. I should have. All the ingredients were there: he was handsome, had a quick mind. He paid attention, and I could trust him. I should have loved him, not Reiner. But that's not what happened.

Drew was set to go to Euell. The grant was secured, housing located, and key observational parameters were set. The rubric and methodology were peer-reviewed.

"It was going to change everything." Drew's words, not mine.

The day he told me about Euell, he looked like he'd been up all night with a fever—skin flushed, tight; and he held his eyes exaggeratedly wide, as if to force them open. He grabbed my arm and hustled me into the grad lounge. "You need to see this," he said, his laptop open, screen showing a map. He pointed to a seemingly random spot. "Euell."

It didn't mean anything to me. It wouldn't have meant anything to anyone.

Drew zoomed in. "Euell. Population 500. Two churches, six bars, and an Eagles' Club. One major employer, Christmas Village, a holiday theme park."

Drew looked at me with those shiny eyes. I nodded encouragingly because I didn't have any idea what he was telling me.

"Star," he said. "There's no crime in Euell." Before I could say anything, Drew faced me, held up his hand. "There should be. It's isolated, on the low side of median income. There's nothing there. Nothing to do. No opportunity beyond this one crazy resort. There should be . . . something. Assaults. Drugs. Theft. Domestic abuse. Gambling. Illegal dumping. Something." He paused. "But there's not. There's nothing."

"Not possible," I said. This was something I knew about.

I am the only legitimate daughter of Rotten Tom Lilly, president of the Pan Lords Motorcycle Club, Falcon Original.

Drew knew it. He'd put it together after Rotten Tom's arrest for racketeering, extortion, arson and homicide, and his face and story were well-documented national news, as well as his plea to his estranged daughter, StarGazer, for reconciliation.

Falcon was a town of 350. It had fewer bars, more churches, and was closer to an urban center than was Euell.

"Someone's keeping the peace. An MC," I said.

Drew shook his head.

"It's a church town?"

He shook his head harder. "No. They have a sheriff. No organized crime. No cults. No gangs of any sort. No groups, in fact, except an Eagles Lodge. The only reported crime in the past 10 years has all been committed by theme park visitors. Or transients passing through."

I didn't know what to say. Crime, deviance in general, was not a single issue with a single solution. It existed in some form wherever there was a group of humans. Any context in which where there was the construction and application of rules.

Drew and I looked back at the map on the screen.

"When do you leave?" I asked.

"As soon as possible," he answered.

* * *

Sometimes the man I love would hold my face in his hands, like he was going to look very deep in my eyes or kiss the top of my head. But instead he'd just look beyond me, at a spot on the wall. Like he was listening. Like he was hearing my thoughts.

Mädchen, hört, und Bübchen!

Sometimes the man I love would take my hand as we were walking. I was proud when he did. Neighbors and townsfolk would look at him, then look at me with him. I saw respect in their eyes.

Macht mir auf das Stübchen!

I should have seen the fear. It was a look, I, more than anyone else, should have recognized.

Bring euch viele Gaben!

People in Falcon had looked at Rotten Tom that way. A tunnel of faces play back, looking down at me with composed smiles, expressions I did not understand. I was just a little girl, holding hands with her daddy.

Sollt euch dran erlaben!

When I was 15, I heard noise in the back shed: Rotten Tom whipping red, and pink, and white, from the backside of Suff Tally, the Pan Lord's third. Rotten Tom looked at me, looking at the ribbons of flesh.

Kling, Glöckchen, kling!

"Like bacon," he said, then smiled at his own joke. "Bacon! From a pig." Tom slapped Tally's torn back with the palm of his hand. "Oink for us, pig!"

Kling, Glöckchen . . .

I ran away from the shed, off the property, down the road, and didn't stop until I reached the elementary school three miles away. I understood all the faces now. I can still hear the agony.

I wonder if Reiner can hear that, when he listens.

klingelingeling!

* * *

Instead of Drew, I went to Euell. The department first tried to sell it to me as honoring Drew's memory. Then, they flat out threatened expulsion if I allowed this research to go outside the department. I was promised the funding would fall like rain. Journal articles *and* the popular media would court me. I'd have a blank check I could just make out to "tenure," wherever I wanted.

"It's just six months, Star," they said.

"OK," I said. I didn't seem to have a choice. "Six months."

The town was a dream. Distilled from then the collective dreams dreamed by anyone who ever dreamed a dream of a small town—where kids rode bikes, Main Street shopkeeps greeted all by name. Friday night socials at Eagles Lodge, where grandparents and teenagers, parents and toddlers all danced together, and then were home by nine.

I moved into the perfect little craftsman intended for Drew. I found fresh-cut flowers in vases set around and a freezer full of casseroles. The utensil drawer even squeaked me a little welcome.

And then he knocked on the door, and let himself in. I was on the hardwood floor, unpacking a box. He came to me and extended his hand. I took it. He helped me up.

His eyes were the pine green of a forest. His features were carved facets in a stone arrowhead. I stood up and, tall, rangy, he towered over me.

I knew who he was, but he introduced himself anyway. "I'm Reiner Lidon," he said. He didn't look like a sheriff. Then he smiled at me, a perfect, pointed smile and wrapped an arm around me, like I was already his. "Welcome home."

There's a line sociologists walk interacting with field work subjects: hovering alongside, a peepshow voyeur. But Reiner, and then the whole of Euell, took that line and tied it into a bow around me, like a wrapped present. In Reiner's arms, that very first moment, he became the man I love.

* * *

The man I love is close now. He is going to find me. He sings slowly, drawing out the syllables.

Hell erglühn die Kerzen . . .

His feet clop like a horse's on the linoleum floor. He opens a cabinet, then closes it again. Clop, clop.

Öffnet mir die Herzen . . .

He plays with me. He opens the utensil drawer, as if I could fit. It squeaks open, then closed. Clop, clop.

Will drin wohnen fröhlich, Frommes Kind, wie selig!

As he clops around the kitchen island, he picks up the tempo. Since I know he knows where I am, I let myself mouth the words of the song: Candles glow in splendor / Hearts are warm and tender / Blessings pure and holy / From the child so lowly.

Kling, Glöckchen . . .

I can feel him outside the door. Like when you sense someone's heat, I can sense his cold. The doorknob turns. Ring, little bell.

klingelingeling!

Ring.

* * *

I spent days observing Christmas Village, dressed as an elf to blend in. Weekends, I greeted the biking children and shopkeeps by name. Friday nights, I danced with Reiner at the lodge. Within a few weeks, he was in my bed by nine.

Aspens turned yellow; the red maples looked like flames. The department wasn't impressed with my notes, my narratives.

"They're stilted. On guard," they said. "Have you built enough trust?"

The department got the grant extended, my leave renewed. "Stay through the new year," they advised. "And return with something."

Reiner wouldn't completely move in. He left a toothbrush, but was careful to leave no other trace, to hurry back to his own house in the purple dawn to shower, shave, and dress for work.

We never fought. But if we had, it would have been about this.

"Everyone knows," I told him. "If you're worried what people would think."

"That's not it, Star," he answered.

"I'd marry you, if you asked. If that's the problem," I said. "If you were wondering."

"I love you, but it isn't right for us to be together," he said. "I have too many secrets." I imagined pain in his eyes as he said this.

"Everyone has secrets." I'd reach for him, to soothe the hurts I saw.

But I couldn't hold him. He had to hold me. I liked that. If I sat very still, his arms would seem to grow around me like the roots of a strange tree.

And as I sat, I was sure that whatever it was, it'd be OK. It'd come to light and it would heal.

He is a good man, I told myself. "You are a good man," I said.

The snows came. Euell was a portrait of winter. Bare trees formed a black net against the sky, cut by creamy pipes of smoke from chimneys. There was so much depth to the shades of frost: milk, opal, maggot, silver, vanilla, faintly blue ice.

In Christmas Village, it was Christmas always. But Euell prepared for the actual holiday with purpose and determination—hanging lights and wreaths, bells and tinsel, mistletoe and pierced luminarias. I never found the source of the aroma of cinnamon and cloves, but it was suddenly there, luscious and unceasing.

At the hanging of the angel atop the town tree, I stood gripped with joy, though Reiner had to answer a call at the park. The carolers wore mufflers trimmed in ermine. Their songs were interrupted by enthusiastic wassailing, calling for toasts, and everyone would hold aloft their cup of cider or eggnog or cocoa.

The librarian tugged gently on my sleeve. I hadn't even seen her next to me, caught up in the spectacle. She looked around, and whispered something. I had to move close to her to hear.

"What are you doing here?" she asked, words clipped and harsh.

I was dumbfounded, then hurt. "It's Christmas Eve," I answered.

"No, I mean, here." She looked around. "We thought you'd be gone by Christmas."

"My project isn't complete," I said. I'd become unwelcome.

"You should get out of here." The librarian was a small woman, and she gripped my wrist then, between my glove and sleeve. Her fingers were strong as they dug in. "You need to go. Now." Then she looked worried. Even seeing only what I wanted, it was unmistakable.

Before I could ask her why, I shivered. Then, I felt another hand on my other shoulder, long enough to stretch from scapula to collar bone. Reiner kissed the back-top of my head. "Hello, Lucinda," he said to the librarian.

She smiled, tightly, rehearsed. "Reiner. Happy to see you. Merry Christmas!" she said, and offered him a cheek to kiss. Afterward, she nodded at both of us, then slipped back into the party, a mosaic of red and green, gold and silver and white, singing in harmony, syncopated movement.

A wassail for a toast. Reiner called out, "Here, here!" Then he turned to me. He slipped off my glove and took my hand in his, then turned to look at the town and the tree. While I hadn't been able to hear the librarian without coming close, Reiner's voice was clear and loud.

"You want truly to be with me?" he asked me.

"Yes," I answered, without hesitation.

He squeezed my hand. "I have a gift for you," he said.

"What is it?" I asked. Delighted, like a child.

As soon as he smiled, snowflakes started to fall. "It's a secret," he said. And the carolers began a new song. Reiner squeezed my hand again. "Oh!" he exclaimed. "This is one of my favorites. Do you know it?"

He didn't see me shake my head because he was already singing along in that surprisingly beautiful tenor. "Ring, little bell, ring!"

* * *

The man I love fills the pantry doorway with his terrible new silhouette. It's not just because he is terrifying that I can hardly look at him; I am shallow and want to see the face and body I came to know, the face and body that belong to that voice, instead of the hooked horns and the goat ears, the red eyes and bulging tongue. He shifts

67

position, hoofs clacking on the linoleum as he waits for my eyes to adjust, then to take him in.

With his claw, he plucks me up and out from behind the pantry shelf, sets me onto the kitchen island.

"I found you," he roars. When he laughs, he raises his head, and his horns scrape plaster from the ceiling. Then, he crouches, sober again, to my eye level. "Why did you hide from me?"

I can't answer him.

"Come sit with me," he says. He picks me up, again, with his claw, but gently. He carries me to the living room, deposits me in a chair.

In the middle of the room, a sack jumps and kicks, rattling the rusted chain that binds it closed.

"What's in there?" I ask, though I'm sure I know.

"It's the wicked," Reiner answers. He sits his great black and red body down onto the sack like a stool.

I hear some screams, some cries. "What do you do with them?"

"I throw them into the fire."

The sounds are familiar. They are agony.

But I don't run away.

The man I love reaches for me with one massive arm, beckoning with his claw. He pats his bent knee. "Come here," he says. "Come and get your gift."

* * *

Caren Gussoff is a SF writer living in Seattle, WA. The author of *Homecoming*, (2000), and *The Wave and Other Stories* (2003), first published by Serpent's Tail/High Risk Books, Gussoff's been published in anthologies by Seal Press, and Prime Books, as well as in *Abyss & Apex, Cabinet des Fées* and *Fantasy Magazine*. She received her MFA from the School of the Art Institute of Chicago, and in 2008, was the Carl Brandon Society's Octavia E. Butler Scholar at Clarion West. Her new novel, *The Birthday Problem*, was published by Pink Narcissus Press in 2014, and her first contact novella, *Three Songs for Roxy*, will be published by Aqueduct Press in 2015. Find her online at @spitkitten, facebook.com/spitkitten, and at spitkitten.com.

The Sixth Night of Krampus:

A VISIT

by Lissa Sloan

Inspiration: Being carried away from home in a basket by a terrifying beast-man, whipped with a birch rod, and possibly receiving heaven knows what other sinister punishments is a harsh consequence for childish wrongdoing. Lissa Sloan wondered what actions would truly deserve such a fate. This question, along with her fondness for 19th century books, inspired "A Visit."

Mr. Pennyrake smiled. He was awfully fond of Christmas. No other time of year offered so many, as he liked to put it, *opportunities*. He admired his new coat in the glass. It was a great improvement on the last one, which that girl Sukie had so carelessly burnt with the iron. She had rather carried on when he had sacked her, sobbing incessantly about her sick widowed mother with an excess of little ones still at home. But he had to make an example of her, or the rest of the servants would think they could be equally careless. And she was much less willing than she had been at the beginning of her employ. So an example was made.

Mr. Pennyrake straightened his cravat. People said he was a handsome fellow, and who was he to argue? With a final approving look in the glass, he picked up his gloves and made his way towards the stairs, where he nearly collided with Jane.

"Beg pardon, sir," she said, blushing prettily and trying to step around him. Like the new coat, Jane was also a great improvement on her predecessor. She was far prettier than Sukie, and Mr. Pennyrake had high hopes of her contributing to his domestic happiness.

"Not at all, my dear," said Mr. Pennyrake, putting out an arm to detain her. "You're in a great hurry."

"It's only Master Henry, sir," she said. "He's wet his bed again, and I must get some clean sheets."

Here Mr. Pennyrake put an arm around Jane's waist and told her he was heartily sorry that Master Henry was causing her extra work and that he would have a word with him this very minute. Jane took a step backwards (her modesty was really quite becoming) and replied that Master Henry was only little and she did not mind, but Mr. Pennyrake insisted on obliging her. Truth be told, he would rather stay and oblige himself with Jane, but Mrs. Pennyrake might be along at any moment, so he promised himself he would make another opportunity later and climbed the stairs to the nursery.

He arrived to find Nurse pulling a clean frock over the young offender's head. "Papa, Papa!" he cried as soon as his head came back into view, and he held out his arms to be picked up. "When is it Christmas?"

Mr. Pennyrake lifted his son, holding him at arm's length for a moment to be sure there was no danger to his new coat. Finding the boy dry, he held him close and carried him over to the nursery fire as Clara dropped her doll and ran to join them. "It's tomorrow, isn't it Papa?" she squealed. "I told him it was."

Mr. Pennyrake nodded and settled himself in the rocking chair with one child on each knee. "It is tomorrow, Clara," said he with a smile. "And what happens on Christmas?"

"Presents!" shouted Henry. "And sweets and oranges and turkey and cake and pudding!" Mr. Pennyrake said nothing, but looked at the children with eyebrows raised.

Clara folded her hands in her lap. "Baby Jesus is born," she said.

"And?" said Mr. Pennyrake. He seemed to have something else in mind.

Henry wrinkled his nose. "We go to church?"

Mr. Pennyrake nodded. "All of those things, but one thing more." He paused for dramatic effect. "Krampus comes visiting."

Little Henry was puzzled. "Who is that?" he asked.

As ever, Clara was ready with an answer. "Our uncle, you ninny," she said in a stage whisper. In this instance, however, she was mistaken.

"No, no," said Mr. Pennyrake with a smile. "Krampus is not a man. Krampus is a beast. He is a beast with tangled black fur, horns like a goat, and a pointed tongue as long as my arm. He walks on two cloven feet. He carries a great basket on his back and a birch rod in his hand. Do you know what those are for?" The children shook their heads, their eyes as large as dinner plates. "The birch rod is for whipping naughty children." Here Henry gasped. "Children who wet their beds at night."

"I told him he mustn't," Clara interjected. "It's the third night this week."

Mr. Pennyrake continued. "Or children who tell tales on their brothers or do not put away their toys." This information silenced Clara at last. "The great basket is for carrying naughty children home with him. What he does with them there I cannot tell you." With that, he deposited both children on the floor. Once there, Clara ran to pick up her doll, and Henry stood contemplating the basket of wet sheets beside his bed, a woeful expression on his face. Mr. Pennyrake strode from the room, a smile on his lips. There was nothing like a little fear to guarantee the desired behavior.

A day full of opportunities awaited Mr. Pennyrake after he left his breakfast table. On the way to his offices he stopped in at a coffee house in the next street but one. Mr. Redfern could be depended upon to be there at that time of the morning, and Mr. Pennyrake had made up his mind to accidentally meet him. Mr. Redfern's round face brightened on seeing Mr. Pennyrake, and he called out to him. "What a surprise to see you," said Mr. Pennyrake as they shook hands.

"Jack," said Mr. Redfern as he gestured towards a chair beside him. "You're the very person I've been hoping to see."

Mr. Pennyrake took the proffered seat. "Oh?" he said. Then, "But you are in mourning. What has happened, my dear fellow?"

Mr. Redfern glanced down at his black armband. "Yes. Well, it's Mrs. Elliot, my aunt."

"I had no idea!" Mr. Pennyrake exclaimed. He had, in fact, heard it from a very reliable source the night before. "My deepest condolences. I'll not disturb you further in this time of grief." He prepared to stand.

Clearly alarmed, Mr. Redfern reached out a hand. "No, no, Jack, don't go. I was hoping you would advise me."

Mr. Pennyrake was all concern. "Now, Redfern, you know I would do anything to help you, but I know nothing of arranging funerals."

Mr. Redfern waved him away. "No, no, Jack. It's about her estate."

Mr. Pennyrake again pretended surprise as Mr. Redfern confessed that he had inherited all of his aunt's money and didn't know the first thing about what to do with it. He had no experience with solicitors and had no idea who to trust with such a sum.

Mr. Pennyrake grasped Mr. Redfern's arm. "You may be easy on that account, Redfern. I would be most happy to advise you." He then explained that he knew of a very promising fund in which he could invest the old lady's money and that he would be happy to make all the arrangements for his friend. Solicitors would charge a ridiculous amount in fees and not take any care that the money was disposed of responsibly. Mr. Pennyrake, however, would handle it all for nothing, save of course some very small expenses he might incur in the course of the business. "If I am not mistaken," he said upon parting, "this may very well be the making of your fortune, Redfern."

As he took his leave, Mr. Pennyrake accepted Mr. Redfern's repeated protestations of gratitude and promises that he would allow Mr. Pennyrake to handle it all. Any charges incurred, Mr. Redfern told him, would be well worth the peace of mind gained by his friend acting on his behalf.

Once Mr. Pennyrake arrived at his offices he made himself as comfortable as any spider in his web and prepared to receive any opportunities that presented themselves. He was not disappointed. First was Mr. Youngson, the grandson and heir of Lord Barrington. It is Christmas indeed, thought Mr. Pennyrake as he stood to welcome his guest, a wide smile on his face. His smile quickly turned to a look of concerned sympathy as the young man related his reason for troubling Mr. Pennyrake.

"I'm afraid I find myself in a bit of a," here Mr. Youngson ran a hand through his hair, "well, an awkward situation. A bit of a fix, really."

Mr. Pennyrake appeared most dismayed to hear it, and offered Mr. Youngson some brandy, which that gentleman readily accepted. "You see," he continued, fortified by the drink, "I sometimes amuse myself with a small bet on a game of cards with friends."

Mr. Pennyrake nodded. "A harmless indulgence, surely," he intoned wisely.

Mr. Youngson pulled absently on his ear and made an attempt at a laugh. It was a feeble attempt, and an even feebler laugh. "That is just what I thought. But now I find I have gone through my entire allowance and have another five months before I receive it again. Lord and Lady Barrington greatly disapprove of gambling, so I can't possibly tell them what's happened to the money or ask for any more. A gentleman of my acquaintance," here Mr. Youngson supplied the gentleman's name, "suggested you might be able to assist me in the amount of," and here he specified a handsome sum.

Mr. Pennyrake made a mental note that the gentleman's kind referral would not go unrewarded. "Certainly, certainly, Mr. Youngson. All you need do is put your name to a promissory note to be due in, shall we say three months?"

Mr. Youngson looked as though he might like to protest, but was not sure how.

"Oh, I know you will not get your next installment for five months, but I do not think I can lend such a sum for so long a time. But perhaps this advance," said Mr. Pennyrake as he wrote out the promissory note, "would allow you to return to your card-playing friends and make up what you have lost."

Mr. Youngson mumbled something about thinking of reforming and not playing cards any more.

"Nonsense, Mr. Youngson," Mr. Pennyrake said bracingly, putting the pen into the young man's hand, "your luck will change, and you can give the business up then if you like."

Mr. Youngson brightened a bit. "Yes," he said, "doubtless it will." He dipped the pen in the inkpot and hovered with his hand above the note. "But what about the terms, for the repayment?"

Mr. Pennyrake made a graceful gesture with his hand. "Oh, they are the simplest in the world. Go ahead and sign the note and I shall provide them to you as you go out. I'm sure you have much to do. You can easily peruse them on your way home." As Mr. Youngson signed his name, Mr. Pennyrake reached in a drawer and lifted out a heavy booklet which he pressed into the gentleman's hand, along with the bank note for the agreed sum. "It's a bit dry reading, to tell the truth. I might not bother if I were you. You will be able to make full payment in three months' time, won't you?"

Mr. Youngson gave a slight movement of the head that might have meant "no" just as easily as "yes."

Mr. Pennyrake smiled broadly and shook Mr. Youngson by the hand. "Splendid," he said. "Then I shouldn't worry with it," he clapped Mr. Youngson on the back as he escorted him to the office door. "Unless of course you ever have trouble sleeping, and then no apothecary could provide you a better remedy."

As it was Christmas Eve, Mr. Pennyrake was especially disposed to be pleased; therefore, everything pleased him. He was pleased to collect payments on debts owed him, along with the generous interest he charged. He was pleased to extend loans (and interest owed) a little longer, knowing that his due would eventually be greater still. He was even pleased to threaten legal proceedings against some who could not pay. He was sorry for them, of course, but they had come to him, after all, and he could hardly be held responsible for the fix they had gotten themselves into.

But nothing pleased Mr. Pennyrake so much as his last visit of the day. It was with a young woman who, with reddened cheeks, told him of her husband's ill-advised speculation in a railroad venture, the poor health which had kept him from working recently, and his ignorance of the seriousness of the situation, as the lady herself handled the family's accounts.

Sitting in the chair he had offered her, she kept her eyes downcast. "He is too proud to accept help from his family, and he would be so angry if he were to find out I had come to you. But our rents are due, and we've no money to pay them, and it is Christmas, and I've nothing to give to the children." At last she had the courage to raise her imploring eyes to Mr. Pennyrake's.

Mr. Pennyrake had to admit he found the lady quite charming. He put on his most concerned expression. "I'm certain I can find a way to help you, Mrs. . . . ." he trailed off, waiting for her to supply her name.

The pink in her cheeks deepened. "I'd rather not," she whispered, her eyes on the floor again.

"Of course, of course," he said sympathetically. "I quite understand this is a matter of some delicacy. In that case I will need some surety of your repayment." Mrs. I'd-Rather-Not seemed to have anticipated this, for, reaching into her pocketbook, she drew out a string of pearls. Mr. Pennyrake smiled. "The very thing," he said, as he bent to make out the paperwork. "Now I will need you to put your name and address to this little paper, but you have my word that I shall not look at it so long as you return with your prompt payment." She nodded.

When the document was finished, she leaned her delicate head over it and studied it minutely. Upon presenting her pen and ink, Mr. Pennyrake discreetly turned his back as she signed, then made a show of folding the paper and sealing it in a way that seemed most secure. Mrs. I'd-Rather-Not would have no way of knowing that Mr. Pennyrake was an expert at un-sealing and re-sealing documents when necessary. At last he slid the payment across his desk and said, "It just remains for me to collect . . ."

She stood, the pearls held to her heart. "They were a wedding gift from my husband," she whispered.

Mr. Pennyrake nodded solemnly. "They will be safe with me, madam, I assure you." She held the pearls out then. He could feel her reluctance through her glove. At last she dropped them into his waiting hand, and she was gone.

Quite, quite charming, Mr. Pennyrake thought to himself as he locked the pearls into his desk. He had a fleeting idea of taking them home to Mrs. Pennyrake, or, even better, to Jane, but he soon dismissed it. He needed those pearls. There was nothing like the need to keep a husband in the dark to turn a Mrs. I'd-Rather-Not into a Mrs. Well-Maybe-Just-This-Once.

As he had decided to leave the pearls, he made a few stops on his walk home, purchasing the requisite brooch, dollhouse furniture, and toy soldiers, not forgetting something special for Jane. Servants deserve to be rewarded for their hard work, after all. Quite satisfied, he arrived home to find his house in the usual pre-holiday disarray. The children were shrieking in anticipation, and the kitchen was a bustle of activity.

"I'm afraid tea won't be ready for a little while yet," said Mrs. Pennyrake, as she tucked a stray curl behind her ear and presented her cheek for a kiss. "They're just finishing the mince pies."

"No matter, my dear," he told her, handing her his hat, but failing to notice the proffered cheek. "Just have Jane bring me a brandy."

His wife made as if to follow him. "I can bring—" she began, but he interrupted her.

"There's no need to wait upon me, my dear. That's what servants are for," he said, leaving her alone with his hat at the bottom of the stair.

In his library, all was quiet. Mr. Pennyrake moved his chair in front of the fire and closed his eyes. It had been a satisfactory day indeed. But it was not over yet. Jane was coming with his brandy, and Mrs. Pennyrake was occupied downstairs supervising the mince pies and the tea. Who knew what might happen? He sighed a contented sigh.

Behind him he heard a rustling. "Ah, Jane," he said with a smile, eyes still closed, "do come in. Close the door behind you." The door did not close. Mr. Pennyrake looked around. "Jane?" No one was there. He settled back into his chair.

A floorboard creaked. "Jane?" There was no response. Perhaps, thought Mr. Pennyrake, one of the children was stealing in to search his pockets for presents. "Henry," he said with a growl, "go downstairs." There was another creak, and a curious odor stole into the room—it was as if the outdoors had gotten in, a scent of cold moist air and freshly turned earth. Mr. Pennyrake found it somewhat distasteful. He did not altogether approve of nature. It was why he lived in town rather than the country. He rose to see if the window was properly fastened. It was. He then closed the door and returned to his chair. Eyes closed, he amused himself by imagining a scene in which Jane entered with his brandy, and he presented her with the pair of gloves he had bought her. He was just arriving at the part in which she unwrapped the package and looked back up at him, eyes shining, when he heard another noise, a clicking on the floor behind his chair. It was like a footstep, and yet not.

Henry would leave the room when he was told, but sometimes Clara showed a decidedly independent tendency to disobey. "Do you remember who comes to visit naughty children, Clara?" Clara would reply when called by name, however, and there was no reply. There was only silence. "Who is there?" Mr. Pennyrake demanded, beginning to feel rather aggrieved.

There was another sound then, a deep rumble, as if a bear had somehow learned to purr. Mr. Pennyrake, about to turn round, suddenly found he was not at all inclined to see who or what was behind him. He asked again, "Who is there?"

The rumble repeated, and the fire seemed to tremble in the grate. There was a voice behind him. "Shall we have a guessing game?" it said. It was an extraordinary voice, like thunder speaking. It sounded as though it came from a mouth unaccustomed to forming words of any sort, let alone English ones. "Someone here has done wrong." Mr. Pennyrake felt a sort of warmth, a presence behind him.

The voice continued. "It is time for my Christmas visit." Now Mr. Pennyrake, frozen to his seat, heard a scraping against the wood of his chair beside his shoulder.

The voice was closer to him now, as was the scent of fur and burning leaves, creeping round his chair like tendrils of fog. "And I am not your uncle."

Mr. Pennyrake vainly searched his thoughts for an appropriate response. Somehow he doubted that telling this creature, whatever it was, that he did not believe in it and had only told his children that story to frighten them into proper behavior would be well received. He fumbled for his handkerchief and wiped the sweat from his cheeks. "Yes, of course," he said, with a bit of a crack in his voice, "I am most indebted to you, to be sure. But I flatter myself I have the matter well in hand."

This time Mr. Pennyrake could feel the vibrations of the wild rumble through his chair. "I am not required," the voice said, only the hint of a question in its inflection.

Mr. Pennyrake was not at all desirous of giving offense to this being. "I am loath to take up your valuable time on such a trivial matter as this, if you take my meaning. I am sure you will forgive . . ." his words were extinguished as he felt his hair being disturbed by a snorting and snuffling all round his head, as if he were the Christmas turkey, being sniffed to see if he were cooked through.

"But I have come," said the voice. "An example must be made."

"It is just what I say myself," said Mr. Pennyrake, and he attempted a chuckle, but it died upon his lips as he saw something he hadn't before. There was a basket, sitting directly next to the fire. He felt quite sure he didn't own a basket so large as that. "But perhaps I could simply tell the children you were here, and there would be no need for that." His arm feebly indicated the basket.

"I will not leave with nothing." The voice was soft, and yet it filled the room. As his mouth was too dry to speak, Mr. Pennyrake took a moment to consider. He eyed the basket, wondering which of his children this creature intended to take. Clara was the most trying to his patience as a rule, but then again, as son and heir, Henry was so far proving a bit of a disappointment. He supposed Mrs. Pennyrake would find it an inconvenience to replace either one of them.

Behind him he could hear the creature breathing. The breaths sounded as if they came from very large lungs indeed. Perhaps it would be best to let the creature make up its own mind. In fact, the basket was sizable enough to hold both children, quite easily. The breathing sound drew closer, as did that animal smell.

Mr. Pennyrake ran his tongue over dry lips. "I'll just fetch them then." He ventured to stand, praying his legs would hold him as far as the door, but a weight on one shoulder pressed him slowly back into his chair, squeezing with an uncanny strength. The sound of the creature's breathing seeped into Mr. Pennyrake's ears and mouth and all the spaces between his clothes and his skin.

The rumble behind him grew so loud Mr. Pennyrake thought (and, be it admitted, ardently hoped) that the noise would rouse the house. "The young will be thoughtless," said the voice. "They will disobey, they may even be naughty. But only those old enough to know better can be truly," the breath was hot on his cheek, smelling of wood smoke and pine forests, "truly wicked." The fire guttered as if a gale were blowing though the room. Mr. Pennyrake began to shrink down into his chair, but he was caught by something sharp and claw-like biting into his shoulders. He sat, immobile, as something warm, wet, and rough dragged itself across his face from chin to eyebrow.

The fire suddenly leapt high and roared in the grate, and for an instant the massive shape of something horned and hairy loomed before Mr. Pennyrake's vision. Then the fire died all at once, as if snuffed like a candle, and Mr. Pennyrake was swallowed by the dark. Now there was nothing but the voice, spreading into his lungs, filling them up until he could barely breathe. "I have not come for your children," it said, lower than a whisper. "I have come for you."

* * *

Mrs. Pennyrake knelt down, surveying her children in their Christmas finery. She straightened Clara's sash and smoothed a lock of Henry's hair from his forehead. Then she gave them each an approving kiss. "Jane will fetch you when all our company has arrived," she told them. "And remember, no asking for presents, but say thank you if you receive any." At this point, the children resumed bounding about the nursery in their excitement as Mrs. Pennyrake descended the stairs, musing to herself. How very changed they both were. Henry had been dry so long she had at last had a pair of short trousers made for him, and he was quite puffed up with the responsibility of being the man of the house. And Clara, too, was growing into a pleasant companion who occasionally let others get a word into the conversation.

Mrs. Pennyrake felt a lightness of heart she could not in any way account for. Everyone had been so kind, that much was true. The servants had done everything they could to ease her mind. Jane in particular had been invaluable. Though she could not explain it, maids had never stayed long in her employ before, especially ones as pretty as Jane. But with Jane managing the house, Mrs. Pennyrake had met the challenges of her husband's mysterious disappearance the best she could. People calling to see her and attempting to pay back money they owed Mr. Pennyrake caused her the most distress. She refused to allow anyone to make her any repayment, for it seemed she had plenty of money, far more, in fact, than she had ever imagined. Truth be told, she began to think she had no idea what sort of occupation her husband had practiced at all. He had always told her he performed a valuable service, but Mrs. Pennyrake could not understand how it could be valuable when these poor individuals came worriedly, even tearfully, to her door to ask, even beg, to be given more time to honor their agreements with her husband.

She had met the most agreeable people in this manner, however. There was Mr. Youngson, for example, who always played at cards, but never gambled. Then there was Mrs. Arbuthnott and her family, who would be arriving any moment now. Mrs. Pennyrake could not think of any reason for a gentleman like her husband to keep a lady's pearls in his desk drawer, and had given them back to Mrs. Arbuthnott straightaway. She was quite happy to promise to say nothing to Mr. Arbuthnott about the matter, and the two ladies had become great friends. Although, and perhaps Mrs. Pennyrake only imagined it, she always felt Mrs. Arbuthnott looked relieved when her inquiries about whether Mr. Pennyrake had been heard of were answered in the negative.

And of course, there was Mr. Redfern. Mr. Redfern had made himself indispensable in every way, helping her with the police inquiry or business matters, dropping round to keep her company, playing with the children; in short, doing any little thing for her happiness and comfort. But still, no one had heard from Mr. Pennyrake since a year ago this very night. No, she could not in any way account for her high spirits.

Mrs. Pennyrake heard the knocker just as she was passing the front door, so she called to Jane that she would answer it herself. There on the doorstep, a happy flush on his round face, was Mr. Redfern. Mrs. Pennyrake begged he should come inside and asked if she could take his hat. He gladly held it out, but did not relinquish it, and their fingers touched over the brim. Neither let go. "You are the first to arrive," she told him. (He always was.) She took a breath, and spoke again. "Before the others arrive," she said, examining his hat intently, "I hope you will allow me to tell you how very grateful I have been for your friendship this past year since . . ." she trailed off. She began again. "You know things have been difficult for us, Mr. Redfern. And I—"

Mr. Redfern pulled his hat a little closer to him and bent his head to the level of hers, hoping for a glimpse of that charming dimple which appeared on her cheek when she smiled. "Charlotte," he said earnestly, "I do despair of you ever calling me Nicholas."

At last she met his gaze, a blush suffusing her cheek. "Nicholas then," she whispered, as she hung his hat on a hook beside the door. "Shall we go up?" As the two proceeded up the stairs to the drawing room, Mrs. Pennyrake smiled, just enough to provoke the appearance of the celebrated dimple, and she allowed Mr. Redfern to draw her arm through his. She was awfully fond of Christmas.

* * *

Lissa Sloan spent a year as book reviewer for *Enchanted Conversation: A Fairy Tale Magazine*. Her poems and short stories are published or forthcoming in *Enchanted Conversation* and *Specter Spectacular II: 13 Deathly Tales*. She also writes and illustrates for younger readers.

The Seventh Night of Krampus:

SANTA CLAUS AND THE LITTLE GIRL WHO LOVED TO SING AND DANCE

by Patrick Evans

Inspiration: The first time Patrick Evans ever heard the name 'Krampus' was in this anthology's call for submissions. It was obvious to him that Krampus was all the anger Santa Claus had been repressing for centuries. Nobody can be that relentlessly nice without eventually snapping and growing claws.

"My name is Kandi Kane and I'm eight years old," she said. Her voice, with its studied lisp, oozed like icing onto a gingerbread house. "I'm a triple threat because I can sing, dance, and act, and everyone says I have perfect comic timing. Comic timing can't be taught, you know."

"My, but you're a big girl, too," Santa said, wincing in pain. Kandi had wrapped her python of an arm around his neck to prevent gravity from dragging her massive body off his lap. His bad hip was like a log in a fire, shot through with crackling red and yellow veins of flame.

It was late November. Santa's mall tour.

Kandi gave him a flat look of frosty condemnation, her bleach-blonde ringlets framing a heavily made-up face whose features seemed altogether too tightly squeezed together into one tiny central region. "You're Santa. You're not allowed to call little girls fat," Kandi said, one eyebrow arching. "You just damaged my self-esteem."

Santa didn't like thinking nasty thoughts but this time he couldn't help himself. The girl's face looked like an arsehole. Literally, an arsehole, a puckering little circle of nastiness in a fat pillow of butt cheek. Santa's guts twisted at the very thought. It was a sign of how far he had fallen that he could make such a cruel observation about a child.

"I haven't eaten a carbohydrate since I was six," Kandi said, "but the fact is I'm big-boned, and big girls only get funny fat-kid supporting roles and that's the tragedy of my existence, because I was born to be a leading lady. So you have to give me double this year for calling me a fatty."

There was no way this kid was eight-years-old. Easily 11 or 12. Too old to be working him in a mall. Santa felt his pulse quicken with anger, and the fog—that infernal fog and the horrors it portended—rolled into his head again. Thickening.

Santa had been assured the fog was purely psychological. But he could actually feel it in his head, filling his skull, tickling the surface until it rolled over the inner surface of his eyes and obscured his vision. And the fog didn't just dull his eyesight. It stole his omniscience. The longer distances were lost and he could no longer see who was naughty or nice. There, in his Enchanted Castle at the Rutherford Plaza, he could barely see the pimply teenage attendants the mall hired, with their skinny long legs in green elf-tights. He could barely see the long bloated lineup of impatient parents and screaming kids.

And then, as he felt Kandi squeeze him harder, pressing her cheek to his and smiling brilliantly, the grey pall over his eyes was torn by three blinding flashes of light in quick succession.

A large woman stood at the foot of his throne. She was an adult version of Kandi. She wore her hair the same way, only her face was lined with age and worry. She was conducting three men, hired professional photographers, who were positioned around the throne. Two standing, one kneeling.

"Smile, Santa," the woman called to him. "Keep smiling. Keep chatting. All very natural." The cameras kept flashing.

Kandi grabbed Santa tighter, snuggling in, smiling brilliantly for the cameras as she spoke.

"You'll be proud of me, Santa, because I don't want any toys for Christmas this year," Kandi said. "All I want is for you to break someone's ankles."

"Ho! You're pulling Santa's beard!"

"Hardly. Cyndy Symmons is the only kid in town who's almost as good as me at jazz-tap, and we're both auditioning for the Home Wholesalers commercial on Boxing Day. But she's anorexic. I would be too if I didn't retain water. The producers will think she's prettier than me and she'll get to play the dancing twist mop and I'll be stuck playing the car tarp."

The fog, recovering from the camera flashes, was thickening again.

Kandi was batting her eyelashes. "You don't want me to be typecast as a car tarp for the rest of my career, do you, Santa, baby?"

Santa blinked his own eyes several times, but he couldn't blink away the fog. "You—you say you want a car tarp for Christmas?"

Kandi's lip, covered in frosted pink lipstick, curled.

"Are you, like, dying of Alzheimer's? I said I want you to break Cyndy Symmons' ankles."

Her voice sweetened again. "I was only going to ask for one ankle, but you called me fat, so now it's two."

Santa was speechless.

"It's only fair, after all. I have a seven octave range and Cyndy only has six." Suddenly Kandi belted out a jingle. "Home Wholesalers—your home is our home toooo!" On the last word she hit a G-sharp seventh that felt like a scalpel piercing Santa's eardrum.

He leapt to his feet, howling in pain, tossing Kandi to the floor. "My scoliosis!" she screamed—in a G-sharp sixth.

Rage squeezed her face down to the size of a pimple as her hand made a rattlesnake strike at Santa's arm. Four long, frosted-pink fingernails dug into the bare skin of his wrist just above his glove. Surely the child was only trying to hoist herself up. But Santa shook her off and staggered back, behind his throne. Kandi crashed down to the floor of the Enchanted Castle again.

Santa had four bloody quarter-moon fingernail marks on his arm.

He ran. He ran through the back door of his cardboard castle and into the mall, shoving shoppers aside in his panic. He threw open the Staff Only door at the far end of the corridor, closing and locking it from the inside.

Dr. Spectra was there. She was eating a watercress sandwich with the crusts removed. Her long, thin fingers, emblematic of her entire frame, were prying open the center spread of a celebrity gossip magazine she'd found on the table, its pages stuck together by the spilled soy sauce of some lunching mall worker. Spectra was Caucasian, but she wore her long brown hair in a Japanese-style double bun. It was her trademark, a carefully cultivated eccentricity, along with her little red satin Chinese slippers and the flowing flower-strewn silk pantsuits she always combined with a billowing flowery silk scarf.

She looked up at Santa, a watercress leaf pasted to her incisors, and said, "What happened?"

"Gnh!" Santa uttered through gritted teeth before gripping his belly in agony and toppling over.

* * *

Months earlier, in late summer, Mrs. Claus had spotted the signs of a relapse on the toy assembly line. Santa had designed an action figure called Sergeant Payback whose gun fired tiny plastic live rounds, and, when disrobed, showed signs of torture by the enemy. L'il Sailor Mouth was a baby doll dressed in a pink sailor's middy top who uttered a different obscenity every time you squeezed her belly.

Santa had no memory of making these toys. He blamed the elves, and in a terrible rage stuffed his three foremen into the cellar freezer for a sentence of 40 years in suspended animation. This left Mrs. Claus unable to access her supply of frozen chicken-flavored soy burgers without having to snap off an elf arm to get at them, which is something a vegetarian would never do.

She sat him down in his den.

"You always get depressed this time of year," she said. "But we both know this is more than your usual funk. *He* wants out. The last time this happened there was no such thing as therapy, so I suppose it was excusable that you laid waste to half of Europe—to say nothing of the upholstery in my sitting room. But nowadays there's no excuse for you not getting help." She marched resolutely to the hallway. He followed her. Two suitcases sat by the door. "I'm tired of begging you to get yourself some proper professional care. I still have nightmares about those damn elves operating on your prostate. And if *he's* coming back, you won't have me to chase after him with a broom and a dustpan. I'm off to stay with Myrtle."

Myrtle was Santa's sister-in-law who had retired to Myrtle Beach so she could be Myrtle of Myrtle Beach. She was constantly on the phone telling Mrs. Claus Santa should be doing more to help out around the house. Santa despised Myrtle. Just hearing her name made him grab his belly and moan.

"See?" Mrs. Claus said. "That's *him* kicking. And I'll bet your head is full of that fog. Hm? Am I right? Of course you'd never admit it. Denial, my dear, isn't just a lake in Egypt."

She made him crazy with her insistence on using clichéd phrases and then getting them wrong.

"It's a *river* in Egypt!" he thundered.

"And now you're in denial about Egypt, too," she said, shaking her head sadly. "I'm leaving Dr. Spectra's business card on the dresser. It's a matter of complete indifference to me whether or not you use it."

She left.

Blast that ungrateful woman, she left!

And after everything he had just had done for her.

Four months ago Santa had torn down the Claus's ancient log cabin on its frigid North Pole ice cap, as well as the rows of wooden toy manufacturing barns and elf barracks. In their place he had erected two 30-story gleaming glass office towers. Tower A housed all the manufacturing and Tower B was residential, with the top four floors going to the Clauses. Santa spent millions on it, and it was all for Mrs. Claus, who had for years complained of drafts in the old house. The day the towers were finished he led her into her very own office with its phone and computer on a vast mahogany desk and an en suite conference room with a table that sat 30. "It's for your knitting!" he said proudly.

"All this for my knitting?" Mrs. Claus said. "Where's my fireplace? And my rocking chair!"

Another 50 million to outfit the offices and living quarters with fireplaces.

Santa told himself he was well rid of her. But the night she left he couldn't sleep without the sound of her snoring beside him—that full-nosed inhalation and twittering exhalation, a duet of pig and bird. And now he was alone with no one to run interference between him and the endless grousing of the elves who despised the new corporate overhaul. Seems they couldn't reach the buttons on the elevators and now had to carry little stools with them wherever they went. What's worse, the towers were designed to withstand the polar winds and shifts in the ice plates by swaying, which meant that in a storm nobody could spear their meat with a fork because their dinner plate was never in the same place long enough. And the rays of Arctic sun, intensified on the mirrored surface of the towers, melted a glacier whose waters flooded Scandinavia. Worst of all there was so much unused space in the buildings that you could go an entire day hearing your boots echo on those cold marble floors without seeing another living soul.

Santa felt foolish. Old. He had ruined everything. And now he was completely, unbearably alone.

He would do anything to have Mrs. Claus back.

The fog in his head grew thicker. The kicking in his belly grew harder. He was scared. In his solitude, in his despair, he could finally admit it. He was so scared his skin had gone whiter than his beard.

Finally he picked up the business card Mrs. Claus had left on their dresser.

* * *

Dr. Spectra was known as the Supernatural Shrink. And she was famous. Who wouldn't be fascinated by her work? Everyone wanted to hear her stories, and she used them to regale the highest of high society. "I'm bound by confidentiality," she always began, and then proceeded to loosen those bounds until they had all but fallen away: "A vampire I treated—let's call him 'Fracula . . .'"

She dined with royalty, tossed her champagne glasses into fountains at Hollywood parties, had her own key to 10 Downing Street, and danced in zero gravity in her very own Space Shuttle launch.

Forever in her mid-30s thanks to access to age-retarding witch's spells and the best Park Avenue plastic surgeons, she had helped hesitant ghosts cross over to the other side, supported vampires as they kicked their blood addictions and switched to iron supplements, traced poltergeists' anger issues back to emotionally absent fathers, told werewolves they were sprouting hair to compensate for weak gender identities, exposed the Invisible Man to his unconscious shame of his own genitalia, and persuaded demons to leave their teenage girl hosts and possess politicians instead because even with a devil inside, politicians couldn't get much worse.

But last year her reputation had gone south when one of her patients, a celebrity ghost who had been a seminal influence on the creation of rock-n-roll, committed suicide after she pushed him too hard, too fast to accept that the dead simply cannot eat cheesecake. Ghost suicides were extremely rare and so difficult to pull off that only the most motivated phantoms ever succeeded. It was a huge scandal.

Spectra's patients fled in droves to her main rival, Dr. Blavatski Conundra, and the invitations to the Oscars after-party, Kosugi camel races, and New Year's Eve at Buckingham Palace faded faster than a mummy's speech impediment after a round of childhood regression.

Mrs. Claus, though, remained a loyal friend. Ten years ago Spectra had helped Mrs. Claus through a mental breakdown in which she thought she was an elf and broke both her baby toes forcing her feet into those curly little elf boots.

When Santa phoned her, Dr. Spectra flew the very next day to the North Pole and hired a dog team to complete her journey from the airport across the miles of glacial ice to Santa's offices. "Phallic overcompensation," she noted as she saw the towers rise up on the horizon.

Every day Spectra laid Santa down on a couch and spoke to him from behind in her slow, soft voice. Santa resented the hell out of her at first. This buttinsky poking away at him, trying to get him to reveal his innermost thoughts—and getting paid a fortune for it too! But after sulking and saying almost nothing for a week he found himself talking, talking as fast as his lips could possibly move. Within a fortnight he came to rely completely on Spectra. She was just so compassionate, so understanding, so validating. He couldn't confess his worries and insecurities and psychic injuries fast enough before their 45-minute sessions ended.

"Nick," Spectra said in one of these sessions, "when you describe how it feels to see the other reindeer taunt Rudolph, I'm reminded of the mistreatment you experienced as an adolescent with a gynecomastia."

"They called me Titty Nicky," he said, sobbing softly. And then, wailing with grief: "St. Titcholas!"

He was in therapy. Deep.

And Spectra's compassion, which had moved him so quickly to trust her, was indeed genuine. It was just as real as her hunger for fame.

Often the two were in conflict. She had always felt guilty turning down desperate clients who were too low-profile to get her name bandied about in the best circles, but turn them down she did. She was fully cognizant of her love of celebrity and had long ago determined it was filling the void left by her emotionally impoverished upbringing, by that traumatic sixteenth birthday when she had asked for a Cadillac and been given a Volkswagen instead. She was less cognizant of some other voids her fame might have been filling, even though she was trained to spot such things. She never married, never successfully dated a man for more than a few weeks. "I'm married to my work," she would say, and for the most part she believed it. But with the world's richest, most powerful, most creative, most beautiful people fascinated by her, desiring her presence—what a wonderful way to fill a void!

When her star sank after the ghost suicide she was desperate to regain that fame. Santa was exactly the high-profile case she needed. But she very quickly came to love the old man, too, for being so fallible, such a mess, really; so ashamed of himself for belying the jolly image by which the rest of the world knew him. She would save this tortured man, so loved by all but so lacking in self-love. Oh yes. The happiness of a man who made children happy would also ensure her own renewed happiness. If everybody won, surely there was no conflict here?

She was convinced from the start that Santa was breaking under the strain of the world's expectation of his perfect goodness.

"Your real self," she said, "is in conflict with the flawless image that for centuries you've tried to live up to."

"It's worse than that," he said cryptically. "If only it were just that."

It took several more weeks before he worked up the courage to tell her.

To tell her about *him*.

About Krampus.

"As I recall, Krampus was a maniac who terrorized half of Europe in the 1800s before disappearing," Spectra said. "It's interesting that you would identify yourself with such a man. The other day when you fired that elf for auctioning two of your sleigh bells on eBay you were perfectly entitled to your anger, Nick. Kicking him in the rump may have been an inappropriate expression of that anger, but it hardly makes you another Krampus."

"No, not 'another' Krampus," Santa said. The fog in his head was thickening. The blood drained from his ruddy cheeks and nose. "The. The Krampus. Krampus was me. At least, he's in me. He lives in me. In my belly. Why do you think that damn ab-workout DVD did nothing to tighten my midsection?"

"Nick, diet and cardio will tighten your abs. Not some gimmick from an infomercial."

"You don't believe me."

"I do believe you," Spectra said. "Full confession. When your wife first called me she mentioned you had, in the past, manifested a second persona. Multiple personalities are rare, but in your case it would be wholly understandable if you created a separate identity to express all of your very human and very understandable feelings of anger and hostility and aggression. Nick, you obviously had a breakdown back in the nineteenth century and ended up mistaking yourself for this psychopath who was rampaging across Europe. You started to believe he was you."

"But Mrs. Claus saw him too."

"You know I adore Mrs. Claus," Spectra said. "But the woman has cataracts and she's incapable of remembering where she put down her glasses. One time she mistook me for Lionel Richie."

Nick stared, frozen, at the wall.

He was silent a long time.

Finally he spoke.

"You really think he's not me?"

"I know it."

"But . . . I feel him kicking to get out. Like last week. At the mall. When that rotten little girl—I mean, that *troubled* little girl—asked me to break her friend's ankles. Krampus was literally trying to kick his way out through my belly."

"Not literally," Spectra said. "Nick, it's no accident that you chose this Krampus person to identify with. Think. What does the name 'Krampus' suggest to you?"

"I—I dunno. What?"

"Krampus. A kicking in your belly. A cramp." Spectra smiled softly. "There's no monster living in your belly, Nick. You're cramping up from all the emotions you're suppressing. And this Krampus persona isn't your enemy. Anger, hostility, aggression—these are emotions that evolved over thousands of years, and they're protective. They tell you when something's wrong, when your boundaries are being crossed. If Krampus represents your anger, then rather than trying to fight him, perhaps you can befriend him instead. Think of him as a friend who's trying, in his own clumsy way, to help you understand your feelings better. And our work here is to integrate the two of you so that there isn't a Santa, and there isn't a Krampus, there's just Nick—a good man with a typically human range of emotions."

"You really think . . . that's possible?" Santa said.

"It's not just possible," Spectra said. "We're going to make that happen. As a team."

Nick could hear the compassion in her voice. And he knew it was sincere. He trusted her.

The fog in his head lifted.

* * *

Over those final weeks leading to Christmas Santa was happy and productive. Every time he felt the fog roll in, the rage kicking inside his stomach, he would say to himself, "Krampus is my friend," and the fog and cramps would subside. Mrs. Claus phoned and said she was proud of him. She said she wished she could come home on the next plane but the abscess on Myrtle's butt cheek had just burst and Mrs. Claus was needed to help her get in and out of her sitz bath.

On Christmas Eve Santa flew laughing into a soft snowfall, the metal of his golden sled flaring like fire in the moonlight, the reindeer jingling, and the chimneys of the world magically slackening, yawning wider and wider for the jolly fat man and his toy sack to slide down.

It was a perfect Christmas Eve.

In the dawn light of Christmas morning Santa was drying his boots by the fire in his den on the 30th floor of Tower B, sipping a celebratory egg nog with Spectra and Warren, his butler elf.

Just then the phone rang.

Assuming it was Mrs. Claus calling to congratulate him, Santa bounded across the floor so fast the room shook.

"I didn't get my present," came the tight little voice over the line.

"Who is this?" Santa said.

"It's Kandi Kane, you fat bastard. Why the hell is Cyndy Symmons still walking?"

"How did you get this number?" Santa said, trying to slow his breathing in that soothing way Spectra had taught him.

"You think I don't have connections?" Kandi replied.

Weeks ago, when Santa had told Spectra what happened the day Kandi sat on his lap at the mall, Spectra said that the little girl was obviously a terribly abused child whose stage-mother—the woman directing no less than three photographers—was robbing her daughter of a childhood to make up for her own frustrated show business ambitions. Knowing this, Santa had taken extra care to leave Kandi something special: a Barbie Dream House, erecting all five stories in the living room and populating it with Barbie and all her friends.

"Little girl. You were given a lovely doll house, for which any child would be very grateful." Santa was practicing the "assertive" voice Spectra had taught him. This was to help him resolve conflict as soon as it arose instead of burying his anger and letting it fester.

"Yeah?" Kandi snarled. "Well Barbie and her friends are now bald and floating face down in the bathtub."

Over the phone Santa could hear a grown woman's voice in the background. "Kandi? Sweetie—your agent says he—well, he says he doesn't take calls on Christmas day."

Kandi lowered the phone and shouted back at her mother.

"And I don't take 'no' on Christmas day or any other damn day, so unless you wanna be floating next to Barbie in the bathtub, get that son of a bitch on speakerphone!"

"I will, I will, Poopykin. Then pancakes!"

"No! Waffles!"

Kandi returned to Santa.

"You've got 'til midnight to break those ankles, fat man. If I lose the twist mop gig at tomorrow's audition, it won't be me who's sorry."

Click.

The sudden brutal kick in Santa's belly made him double over and fall to the floor in agony, toppling the phone stand and shattering the glass winter-scene snowball that sat beside it. Mrs. Claus' favorite.

* * *

Dr. Spectra had Santa tear apart a feather pillow with a crude drawing of a little girl's face on it. Then they did their breathing exercises. Then they chuckled at how wonderfully human we all are to react so powerfully to people like Kandi, who do nothing to deserve such a large helping of our thoughts and feelings.

That made the kicking stop. Santa's mood picked up through the day and he laughed that night in his old booming way, sitting at the head of the table and carving the Christmas turkey for Spectra and all the elves.

And then on December 28th, just after sundown, a polar storm started moving in. When Santa didn't come to their therapy session,

Spectra found him down in the lobby of Tower B, staring grimly through the glass doors.

"I hear dogs," he said.

"Dogs?"

"A sled team."

Spectra listened. "I don't hear anything."

"My omniscience may not be what it used to be, but I can still hear dogs a mile off. Someone's coming."

"In this storm?"

"Storm's just starting. They'll make it."

Sure enough, ten minutes later, Spectra could hear the dogs barking too. Soon then they emerged into view, a team of 12 huskies pulling a golden sled with a woman in a blue parka working the reins. The drawstring of her hood was pulled tight around her suffering red face, lacerated by wind and snow, with storm-drawn tears frozen on her cheeks. Beside her sat a plump little figure in a white hooded cape with a gold trim. As the dogs halted in the nimbus of light emitted by the tower lobby, Santa recognized Kandi's mother. And inside that white hood, the tiny, cruel face of . . .

No. It couldn't be.

He staggered back a step.

"Nick?" Spectra put her hand on his shoulder. "Who is it, Nick?"

He shook his head over and over, grabbing his belly in pain.

Kandi and her mother disembarked. Kandi's mother pushed open the lobby door and held it for Kandi who walked imperiously inside and stood in front of Santa.

"You had your chance, fat man," Kandi said. "I was a good girl all year and I asked you for one damn thing and you didn't give it to me. Cyndy Symmons landed the dancing twist mop role in the Home Wholesalers audition." She poked him in the belly. "I told you you'd be sorry. And I meant it."

* * *

In the big chairs around the fire in the den they were joined by Warren, who served everyone a huge mug of hot chocolate.

"Now one of the best ways of really talking something out," Spectra said with a warm and ever-so-slightly condescending smile, "is to try our best to validate what each of us is saying and feeling. For example: Kandi, I'm hearing that you feel a lot of anger and disappointment that you didn't get what you wanted for Christmas, and that makes me feel sad."

Kandi calmly sipped her hot chocolate and winced. She handed the mug to her mother.

"Blow on it."

Her mother, with trembling hands, took the mug and started to blow.

"Okay," Kandi said to Spectra. "What I'm feeling is that I want to puke just looking at that outfit you're wearing. If I spend any more time around your stupid floral prints I'm gonna need a hay fever injection. So why don't you and your feelings and your stupid flowers just screw the hell off?"

Santa, furious, tried to jump to his feet. Spectra, seated beside him, pulled him back down. "No, Nick," she said firmly. "An angry reaction is exactly what she wants."

Spectra turned to Kandi's mother. "Darla. Kandi is obviously a very troubled young lady. Have you ever sought counseling for—"

"Has she ever!" Kandi cut in with a cruel laugh. "But the joke's on her. Dr. Richards is on my side and says Mommy has to do more to be supportive of my gifts."

"It's true," Darla said in a trembling voice. "Dr. Richards says I'm far too controlling."

"I didn't tell you to stop blowing!" Kandi barked.

This little girl wasn't making it easy, but Spectra was determined to model healthy communication skills for Nick.

"Kandi, you've said some hurtful things tonight," Spectra said. "I need to lay some boundaries here. While you're a guest in this home you can either treat all of us with respect, or you can leave."

"It's not your home, Potpourri," Kandi sneered. "And my business is with tubbo here."

Spectra was going to try again to lay those boundaries, but Santa placed his hand on her wrist. "Let her speak. I'm okay." He winced once in terrible pain, a sure sign of kicking in his belly, but then his face went calm. "You've come a long way to talk to me, little girl. So say your piece."

"You wanna hear my piece?" Kandi smiled darkly, and then, in the very next moment, her eyes erupted in tears. She spoke in a small, frightened voice. "I'm scared if I say anything the big mean fat man will come back. He knows where I live. He said he *watches* me when I'm asleep!"

Reaching into her mother's purse she pulled out a little rag doll. Her finger started pointing to various areas on the doll's body.

"He touched me here," she said slowly, and then, with gathering speed, "and here. And here and here and here." Kandi rubbed her eyes. "Yes, thank you, officer. I would like a lollipop."

She tossed the doll to the floor, crossed her legs, and smiled.

Santa nodded. "I see. You're threatening me." He pointed at the rag doll. "With this." And then his voice roared with a fury so sudden and violent that Spectra, Warren, and Darla all jumped in unison. "With this!"

"Nick, she's a sick, troubled little girl!" Spectra implored.

"Oh, Santa, cutie," Kandi said. "I'm not threatening you now. You got your threat back in November, at the mall. Me and Mommy filed the police report as soon as we left your Enchanted Castle. We were laying a bit of groundwork in case I ever had a reason to get even with you." She smiled, ever so sweetly. "Remember when I sank my fingernails into your wrist? When you tossed me off your lap? The cops were scraping out DNA samples and photographing my bruised bum an hour later. But, see, I was just too *terrified* of the big, bad man to give them your name."

She stood up, strode forward, placed her hands on the armrests of Santa's chair, and leaned in so close their noses were almost touching.

"Until today," she said. "I reckon the cops will set out as soon as the storm lets up." Then she straightened again, yanked her hot chocolate away from Darla, and returned to her seat. "I timed my call to the police so they'd be delayed by the storm. I wanted a chance to see you before the cops got here with their DNA kits. I wanted to get a good long look at your stupid face when you heard what's coming."

She sipped her hot chocolate.

"You're through, Santa. Washed up. It's *over*, fatso. And all because you were too damn selfish to make one beautiful little girl's Christmas dream come true."

Spectra looked at Santa. The look on his face frightened her. It was all wrong. He wasn't angry. He wasn't scared. He appeared to be in a state of complete serenity. And he wore just the faintest smile.

"Nick . . . ."

"Spectra," he said. "I'm fine. Really. It was like this the last time. In Europe, 1871. The pain in my belly finally just stops, and I feel this tremendous sense of peace as if—well, as if I've died. Like my body and my troubles are no longer my own." He closed his eyes, blissfully. "Krampus is my friend." He sighed. "I think, perhaps, you'd had better run, Spectra, dear."

And then she saw it. A foot. No—a hoof. A hoof pushing outwards from inside the ample flesh of Santa's belly, popping open his coat and rolling his white undershirt up to his nipples. It was extending his belly, stretching it thinner and thinner until the skin seemed shrink-wrapped over the hoof.

"What the hell's he doing?" Kandi said. "Does he know how disgusting this looks?"

The hoof, so clearly delineated under Santa's skin, protruded a full two feet now. Santa's navel looked ready to tear open. His eyes opened a crack. They were rolled to the back of his head so that only a sliver of the whites showed. Spectra recognized the rapid eye movement of a sleeper. She hesitated, then grabbed Santa's forearm and shook it to rouse him. "Nick! Nick! Wake up!"

Warren had seen enough. He hopped to his feet.

"Folks, it's been a pleasure knowing you," he said. "I'll be hiding in the dumbwaiter, which I'm delighted to say, Miss Kandi, your ass could never squeeze into."

With that he ran from the room.

The hoof straining against Santa's belly was now kicking wildly inside its sheath of skin.

"Will someone tell me what the hell's going on?" Kandi said. She remained seated, still holding her hot chocolate. Her mother was standing now, backing against the brick facade that arched over the fireplace.

Another hoof appeared: this one in Santa's throat. As it stretched through his many chins his head fell back like a Pez dispenser. A log in the fireplace made a loud cracking noise and again Spectra jumped in her seat. But was it a log? Or had the old man's neck just snapped? That hoof forcing Santa's head back—all the way back to his shoulder blades now—must have broken his neck. So was he dead? Was Santa Claus dead? His arms hung limp at his side, his limp knees turned inward.

And then with a bang so loud the windows shattered and the storm came roaring in, Santa's entire body blew backwards, knocking his chair back, and landing in the shadows just outside the circle of firelight in which they all sat. All that was left of him over there in the dark was a jumbled mound of red wool and white fur trim, and, jutting ceiling-ward, the wiry hairs of a thick white beard.

Krampus landed in a ball on the floor in front of the fire. At first all Spectra could discern was a huge black rounded mass soaked in a reeking pearly-white ooze. The smell of it! She knew that smell—the sickening smell of infection. Yes, it was pus. And fat. The creature was covered in pus and fat!

Krampus began to laugh as he rose, a coarse, dark baritone mockery of Santa's laugh. "Ho! Ho! Ho!" His black mane was lifting like an angry cat's fur, still sodden with that stinking ooze, and then he paused halfway up, arched his back, and shook like a wet dog, showering the onlookers with his wretched, stinking slime.

He continued rising. It seemed to take forever for him to stretch his cramped muscles out to their full length, but when he did he stood 10 feet tall under the tower's 12-foot ceilings. He had the legs of a satyr and the upper body of an impossibly muscular man. His face, though covered in black fur, was a hybrid of jungle cat and human. His fur was the length of a shaggy cat's except along his spine where it grew in a thick mane so long and tangled and clotted with fat and pus that it formed dreadlocks cracking like whips with every move he made. His eyes were barely visible, long thin slits that allowed the faintest glow of blood-red light to escape. He stood looking down at the group, swaying slightly from the uncertainty of his own limbs after being balled up in a fat man's torso for so long. He ran the four powerful long fingers of his left hand down the length of his arm, gathering a sticky thick wad of ooze from his fur. He then released a 10-inch tongue from his mouth which hungrily lapped the gobs of pus and fat from his fingers.

His glance moving from chair to chair, the monster spoke. His words, long and sandpaper rough, were charged with an irrepressible black joy.

"I would see you better," he said.

And with that the fur on his forehead parted. A giant third eye was released, bulging now from his forehead. If it weren't for the long lashes above it no one present would have understood that this was indeed an eye because there was no iris, no white, and its surface wasn't smooth. It was a jaundiced yellow and honeycombed like a beehive.

"Better," he growled. "Eye to see you. Now. Horns."

And so his horns erupted. Two fat grey-black horns burst from his temples with the sickening sound of a skull cracking open. Quickly they thickened, nourished from some furnace of energy inside the monster, and curled into two giant ram's horns, each of which was larger than the head from which they had sprouted. Then more cracking sounds. Spectra, Kandi, and Darla could see movement under the skin of the creature's forearms. Two thick protuberances made of the same stuff as his horns suddenly erupted through his wrists. They extended a foot and half past his knuckles and their points were as sharp as spears. His eye, that honeycombed orb, moved to and fro, proudly surveying these terrible weapons his arms had produced. His wheezing breath was heavy with anticipation.

Krampus closed his third eye and sniffed at the air. His black lips broke open in a long smile that revealed a set of razor-sharp teeth, every one of them an inch-long yellowed incisor.

"I smell . . . candy . . ." he said, and took a single step forward to the chair where Kandi sat. His third eye opened. "There's my Kandi!" He took in a long, great breath of air, and shivered with pleasure. He shook his long, clawed index finger at the girl, the spear-horn on his forearm slashing at the air with every movement of his hand.

"Naughty. Not nice."

"You don't scare me," Kandi said with a calm that was almost as chilling as the joy in the creature's husky, murderous utterances. "My mommy's here, and any parent would die before she allowed her little girl to get hurt."

Krampus turned to Darla, still pressed against the fireplace.

"Hello," Darla said in a squeaky little voice.

The monster smiled again.

"Kandi, honey," Darla said, edging along the wall, her voice squeaking higher with every word. "Make sure your phone is turned on so I can reach you."

Then she bolted from the room.

"Oh, fine," Kandi said, rising calmly from her chair as Krampus, snorting with glee, turned back to her.

And then her face erupted with a rage like a boiling, bubbling vat of porridge.

"You think you're tough?" she yelled. "I've negotiated residuals with advertising execs who eat cat-faced monsters like you for breakfast!"

She flung her hot chocolate into Krampus' third eye. He closed it, staggered back, burying his face in his hands and howling in pain and rage.

Throughout all this Spectra's terror had frozen her to the seat of her chair. But this sudden eruption of violence—initiated, unexpectedly, by Kandi—had a bracing effect. She leapt to her feet. Krampus' horrible third eye opened again and he drove the spear on his arm forward, in Kandi's direction. Somehow Spectra was faster. She pulled Kandi out of the way and the monster's spear pierced the seat the girl had recently vacated, impaling it so deeply that his hand was buried to the wrist in the chair back. He lifted his arm, chair and all, and shook it high and low around the room until his arm spear, through the chair back, pierced one of the oval track lights embedded in the ceiling. He convulsed with an electrical shock, roaring furiously.

What Spectra desperately wanted to do now was abandon Kandi and find somewhere to hide while Krampus tore the little brat to pieces. But she couldn't. Terrified as she was, Spectra just didn't have it in her to allow a child to be murdered. What's more, she knew that if there was even the slightest chance that Nick could somehow reverse this transformation, he'd be destroyed by the memory of murdering a little girl, even one as despicable as Kandi. Nick needed Spectra more now than ever before. He needed protecting from himself.

Spectra grabbed Kandi's hand. "Run!"

Out of the den and down the hall they ran. Spectra was pulling Kandi in the direction of a door marked "Stairs" when Kandi broke free of her and ran farther down the hall to the elevator. She pressed the down button.

"There's no time for that," Spectra screamed.

"It's on this floor, you mouth breather!" Kandi said, pointing to the row of numbered lights running over top of the doors. The elevator opened immediately and Kandi ran in, pressing the ground floor button a dozen times. Spectra raced after her, leaping through the doors just as they were closing. The elevator's motion detector, registering Spectra's body, opened the doors wide again, and the woman and girl stood inside, waiting. Suddenly the entire tower shook. Krampus had finally freed himself, hurling the chair off his hand and across the den with a terrible crash.

Just as the elevator doors began to close again, Spectra stuck her head out to look around the corner. She saw that the damaged chair had gotten stuck in the doorframe of the den and was jutting out into the hall.

"Get your damn head out of the door!" Kandi yelled. Too late. Spectra had again triggered the motion detectors and the doors fully opened once more.

"I'm sorry! I'm sorry!" Spectra cried.

The doors were sliding shut a second time when again the tower shook, this time with the shock of Krampus' mighty leg kicking the chair through the doorframe, propelling it into the hallway wall where it shattered into a mangled mass of wood and fabric. He emerged roaring from the den. Once again Spectra stuck her head out of the elevator to look. And once again the motion detector opened the doors wide.

"He's coming!" Spectra screamed.

"Are you on drugs, lady?" Kandi grabbed Spectra's floral silk scarf and pulled her back into the elevator. She coiled the scarf around her hand over and over until there was no slack and Spectra was brought to heel, choking and kicking on the elevator floor. They could hear Krampus' hooves thundering their way.

"You never seen a horror movie, retard?" Kandi said. "Just watch. He's gonna get his goddamn hand in the doors before they close."

The doors slid shut. Kandi let go of the scarf.

"Or maybe not," Kandi said, shrugging as Spectra scrambled to her feet.

And then came an explosive force that knocked them both against the far wall: Krampus' fist punched right through the elevator's metal doors. His arm spear managed to skewer one of Spectra's buns, lifting her off her feet as the lift began to descend. She was carried to the ceiling, the horn slicing upwards through the metal as the elevator dropped.

The horn sliced right through the ceiling, ripping the entire bun from Spectra's skull, until finally Krampus was forced to withdraw his arm. Spectra crashed down to the elevator floor.

The lights on the control panel showed the floors counting down as the torn metal on the door screeched and blew sparks along the concrete surface of the elevator shaft: 30. 29. 25. 20. 17.

Kandi let out a labored, breathy chuckle of relief. "Sayonara, stinky."

"Sayonara stinky?" Spectra sobbed. "Sayonara us! Are we supposed to run outside? If he doesn't kill us the storm will!"

"We'll cut open a couple of the huskies from my sled team and climb inside. Like in Empire Strikes Back."

"I can't fit inside a husky!"

"Then gut a reindeer! Why am I coming up with all the answers? I'm a kid!"

Then, just as the elevator passed the third floor, it shook violently and came to a halt.

"Oh, crap," Kandi said.

All was still for a moment. Then the elevator shook and began to ascend again in a series of violent jerks that forced the woman and girl to the floor.

"We—we're going up," Spectra gasped, as Kandi's little finger stabbed wildly at every button on the panel.

Krampus was pulling them back, pulling the whole elevator up by its cables like fish on a line. They could hear slackening coils of elevator cable crashing onto the ceiling as he closed the distance between them.

One final great yank and they were back on the 30th floor. They watched as Krampus' giant fingers reached into the hole he had made in the doors and ripped them right out of their frame accompanied by the deafening scream of tearing metal. Tossing both panels to either side of him, he stood, his breath slightly labored, emitting a grunting, snorting laughter. They were trapped. They were his, now.

Spectra fell back against the elevator wall and slid to the floor, screaming. Kandi did not. She strode forward to the monster and calmly pointed at his prodigiously exposed genitals.

"You ever considered a loincloth, Tarzan?"

And then her body dipped back and off to the side. Her foot shot upwards, and with a "KEE-YA!" she nailed him, hard, right in the balls. Krampus grabbed himself and collapsed onto the floor, howling in pain and rage. "*Kung-Fu Princess*, asshole! I trained four months and puked off 20lbs for that and who got the part?"

She jumped, landing both feet on Krampus' left horn. It made a slight cracking sound on impact. "Cyndy Symmons!" Kandi shrieked.

Krampus clambered to his knees and was about to stand up when Kandi dropped him once again, this time with a piercing sustained G Sharp Seventh, which made both the monster and Spectra curl into fetal positions, covering their ears. Kandi turned to Spectra in the elevator. "Yo! Prescription Pad!" She kicked her. "Let's go!"

Now it was Kandi who took Spectra by the hand. As Krampus roared and rolled in pain they ran down the corridor and turned a corner. At the end of this new corridor they saw another "Stairs" sign over another doorway. As they pulled the door open they could hear Krampus getting back onto his feet and running after them. The floor jumped and the walls hummed with the force of his hoof-falls.

Kandi ascended the first few stairs. Spectra tore her hand free. "The roof? We can't go up there!" she said. "We'll be trapped!"

"Duh! He'll think we went down!"

Kandi was already up the first flight of stairs and turning on the landing as Spectra began mounting the stairs after her. On the landing she paused to look back just as Krampus arrived at the door. He saw her. He knew they were headed for the roof.

At the speed he was going he crashed into the doorframe, which was too small for him, but with both hands pressed against it, and with no greater exertion than if he were opening curtains, he forced the frame open wide, the metal contorting and the cement of the firewall around it exploding in a cloud of dust and concrete shrapnel.

But Kandi and Spectra were able to climb faster than Krampus, whose hooves were too big to fit cleanly on the steps. He would run up a few, then lose his balance and skip down a few, bellowing with rage.

Kandi and Spectra arrived at a door marked "Roof." Kandi threw it open. Immediately a powerful gust of wind and snow blasted her, but she pushed on through it, disappearing into a whipping, roaring cloud of white.

Again, Spectra hesitated. The whole building shook with the sounds of Krampus charging up the stairs. He would appear any second. But that polar storm was lethal. For a moment she considered surrendering, begging for mercy, imploring any trace of Nick that might still exist in the creature to spare her. And why not? She had only ever, ever been his friend.

No. She was Nick's friend, not the monster's. In every therapy session she had taught Santa how to thwart this monster that was kicking for freedom inside of him.

Spectra ran through the door onto the roof, into the white rage of the storm. In a silk pantsuit she'd last five minutes out here, if she was lucky. But as she lifted each leg high to plant her foot down in the deep snow (no hope of running in the stuff) she was surprised to find her terror slowly receding the farther out into the storm she went. Even as her body temperature plummeted she had the strangest sensation of a profusion of peace suddenly flowering in her heart, overflowing and warming her from the inside out.

With nothing to look at but a screen of snow, her vision turned inwards to an image of herself sitting at some long, beautiful library table with a thick, hardbound textbook open before her. She was turning the pages, researching her own current state of mind. Either the storm was slowly killing her and this loss of fear, this sudden feeling of peace, represented the gradual shutting down of her nervous system, or this feeling was psychological, a moment of great significance, an epiphany that she hadn't fully realized until now she very much needed. There was a clinical name for this, but she couldn't find it in this enormous textbook, and she was losing interest in even trying.

It troubled her, just a little, that her survival instinct seemed to have quit on her. But there was something bracing in the grandiosity of the storm, in having fled to the top of a building on the top of the world with not one but two obliterating forces of nature upon her—Krampus and the storm. She closed the book in her mind. A sudden rush of sadness: she pictured herself leaving the North Pole having fully cured Nick, going back to Europe and Hollywood for a resumption of the parties, the awed celebrities and dignitaries lining up to hear her stories—Spectra, the great supernatural psychiatrist. Everyone talking about her latest triumph. "The shrink who saved Santa Claus!"

The attention. The validation.

And then she asked herself if she could say goodbye to all that, if she could settle once and for all which was more important to her: the celebrity or the work itself. And if it was indeed the work, then she had a job to finish up here on the top of the world. A child was out there somewhere, in need of protection, even if she was the most despicable little brat who ever drew breath. And Spectra's client was out there too, a good man, the best man ever, desperately needing protection from himself.

She couldn't feel the storm at all anymore. The light, airy, flowing flowery clothes that Kandi had mocked now became an external representation of the grace and beauty and lightness and goodness of her being.

And then the winds, as if she had commanded them—and maybe she had—took a sharp turn, interrupting for moment the storm's blinding cyclonic white-out effect and forcing it sideways in straight lines. For the first time she could make out what was happening on the roof. She saw Krampus first. The storm was so thick that he had passed her without either of them knowing it. He was closing in on Kandi, who stood 15 feet from the edge of the roof, facing the other tower. Kandi began to run for the edge of the building. She had her arms up in a dancer's posture and was clearly about to risk everything on a single dancer's leap over the abyss to the adjacent roof.

One chance in a million the girl would make it, Spectra thought. But one chance was better than none at all.

Krampus was laughing, charging after Kandi.

Krampus, with his length and power, would almost certainly make the jump.

And so Spectra charged after him.

Kandi leaped, one leg stretched forward and the other back in a ballerina's grand jeté. Laughing wildly, Krampus leaped after her. And Spectra, borne aloft by that flowering grace and beauty and lightness of soul, leaped too. In mid-air between the towers she reached for Krampus. She caught him, wrapping her arms around his lower legs. She squeezed. Her grip, with those skinny arms of hers, was unbelievably strong. Krampus was unable to kick, unable to use his legs to muscle his massive bulk across the gulf.

A sudden, perfectly timed updraft lifted Kandi over the gap between buildings and set her down on the other tower. This same wind was not equal to the task of carrying Krampus, especially not with Spectra holding onto him. The second tower was just an inch beyond his reach as he began his downward plummet. While Krampus howled, he and Spectra disappeared into the snow between the two towers, into the whipping wind which seemed to score the surface of reality itself.

And in a dark corner of the den, Santa's abandoned suit stirred. The great mound of red wool and white fur began to deflate like a tent whose supports had suddenly been pulled. The white beard, jutting out over the suit, and all the white fur trimmings twisted and crackled and curled away as if they were burning—but there was no flame. The red wool of Santa's suit broke apart into little bits and these little bits paled and turned rough and dry like pencil shavings, curling in on themselves. Eventually the curls grew so tight they vanished altogether, leaving just a fine coat of dust on the floor.

Krampus had fallen to his death between the towers. And the other man he was, his good self, would not rise again.

* * *

Kandi found the stairwell door on the roof of Tower A and hurried inside. She went downstairs and looked around for someone to yell at. There was no sign of any elves on the floors she searched. Or her mother.

The police would be coming after the storm died down. That gave her a bit of time to snoop around for anything of value. She searched offices and work rooms and private quarters, emptied drawers and trunks and wardrobes, and then finally she came across Santa's papers in a lockbox that the trusting old man had never bothered to lock. It was full of bank statements, bonds, flyers listing terms and conditions for countless accounts and investments. The old guy had some big money backing his operation. International investors. Hedge funds. Futures. Best of all was an agreement with something called The Bank of Eternal Youth. A monthly debit from Santa's savings account in exchange for never aging a day.

A goddamn goldmine.

This, then, is the story of how Kandi Kane and her seven tiny reindeer came to bring gifts to all the children of the world every Christmas Eve, and how she leveraged this gig so that the rest of the year she starred in heart-warming Hollywood movies about a spunky, cute plump girl, singing and dancing, forever young, forever stinking rich and famous.

Kandi's lawyers kept Mrs. Claus at bay, kept her, year after year, on the pull-out bed in her sister Myrtle's Myrtle Beach bungalow.

And Cyndy Symmons was jumped in an alley by four very small men who wore curly-toed boots and jingling bells on their hats. Her broken ankles recovered enough that she could walk with the aid of a cane, but she never danced again. She's 40 now, working as a script-reader at Paramount. And, it has to be said, she's not aging well.

To all of which Kandi Kane says, "Ho! Ho! Ho!"

* * *

Patrick Evans is a fiction writer and journalist who has recently published short stories in the anthologies *Age of Certainty* and *Fresh Blood*. In 2013, after four decades in Toronto, Canada, he moved to the United Kingdom because he genuinely prefers rain to sun.

The Eighth Night of Krampus:

BETWEEN THE EYES

by Guy Burtenshaw

Inspiration: "Between The Eyes" takes place in towns that the author knows well. The story was inspired by and reflects the high levels of stress caused by modern life, and how there is always a price to pay for every decision you make. Sometimes you get through, but other times you just crash and burn.

"If you were going to die and you were given a choice of being shot between the eyes or being covered in petrol and burnt, what would you choose?"

Mervin looked up from his pint of Blackhorse ale and turned his head to stare at the man who had been wittering away for what felt like a lifetime.

Mervin had gone to the pub with the intention of downing so much alcohol he would not just forget the week he had just endured, but the entire year.

Mervin regarded the man through his blurry eyes and, without thinking too hard, said, "Bullet between the eyes."

"Popular choice," the man told him. "But what if the bullet between the eyes was scheduled for first light and the fire was for first light exactly one year from now?"

Mervin had trouble focusing on the man's face. An unkempt black beard seemed to fill his face. Horns protruded from the side of his head, curling up into a haze, and fading into nothing. He looked away and screwed his eyes tightly shut, and then opened them and focused on the beer mat on the bar to clear his head.

"What are you on about?" Mervin asked wishing the man would go away and leave him in peace.

"One whole year. Think of all the greatness you could achieve in one year knowing that was all you had."

"Bullet is quicker," Mervin said.

"But sooner, and fire isn't so bad. The smoke gets you before the flames, and there's a whole year before it happens."

"Okay, okay, I'll take the fire if you'll just leave me alone."

Mervin realized he had raised his voice a little higher than intended, and people were staring at him.

Someone tapped him on the shoulder and he turned to see Ben Mudd, the barman, staring at him. "I think you've had enough."

"I've only just started," Mervin told him suddenly feeling strangely sober.

"And now you've just finished."

"I say when I'm finished. Another pint and whatever my friend here is having."

Mervin turned, his drunken smile drooping when he saw the empty bar stool next to him.

"What's his name?" Ben asked. "Don't tell me, it's the invisible Santa, and what will his little helpers be having?"

Mervin looked around the bar, his eyes struggling to focus, and then he found himself lying on the hard wooden floor staring up at Ben as he leaned over the bar.

"Now I've had enough," Mervin mumbled as a dull pain started to build between his eyes.

* * *

Mervin opened his eyes and stared into the darkness. For a brief moment he felt afraid, and then he recognized the spherical white light shade hanging from the ceiling.

He could not remember getting home. He had a hazy recollection of sitting at a bar. Someone had been talking to him and then he had fallen over.

His head was pounding, the pain worst between his eyes. He sat up and massaged his forehead with his thumb, the pain easing when he pressed hard with his thumb and returning when he stopped. The time on the clock on his bedside table was half past seven.

Water. He felt thirsty. He felt for the cord next to the bed and turned the bedside lamp on. The light from the bulb felt far too bright, but it banished the darkest shadows, and the aching in his eyes seemed like a small price to pay.

He swung his legs over the edge of the bed and looked down at the clothes he vaguely recalled putting on the previous morning. His shirt was severely creased, but that did not bother him. It was not as if he would be entertaining anyone over the Christmas holiday.

He smiled and wondered how, when you were no longer working, you could tell when the Christmas holiday started and when it finished.

He suddenly had a craving for a smoke. He looked at his bedside table. There were none there. He patted his pockets, but all he felt was his wallet.

He stood and walked to the kitchen where he turned the tap on and leant down to drink direct from the spout. He drank until his thirst was satiated and turned the tap off standing to face the window.

It was still dark outside, but he knew the sun would soon be making an appearance. He took a deep breath of air hoping it would quell his craving for nicotine, but his habit refused to be beaten so easily. There was a petrol station about a mile away, and if there was one place that would sell cigarettes at half past seven in the morning on Christmas Day, that was the place to be.

* * *

He opened the front door and shivered as a cold breeze hit him. He took a deep breath of the outside air and pulled the door closed behind him as he stepped into the outside world. He checked his watch. It was a quarter to eight.

The sky to the east was a pale gray, but all the houses were still in darkness. He knew it would not be long before lights started to turn on across town with over-excited people sitting around their decorated trees tearing paper from presents.

There had been a time when Mervin had been one of those people, but not anymore. His girlfriend had left him when he had been promoted and his hours grew longer, his parents had both been killed in a car accident in France shortly after, and, apart from a reclusive uncle in New Zealand, he had no relatives.

As he walked along the road he found himself wondering whether life could get any more depressing. He knew that it could and probably would. He had thought the same the week before, and had decided he had reached the bottom when he had been handed a letter informing him that he was surplus to requirement. The pay had been exceptional, but the contract had been temporary, and a clause had allowed termination with only a week's notice. His manager Robert Selwyn had seemed to take great pleasure in highlighting the clause to him before escorting him out of the building.

The walk to the petrol station was a lonely one. There were usually people making their way to the station at Walthamstow Central, but Christmas Day had everyone confined to their homes.

At the petrol station a non-descript person clad in black leathers, face concealed by the dark visor of a black helmet, was just moving away from a pump. The engine of the motorbike revved loudly as it sped away as though to tell the world the dawn was approaching.

A wave of warm air greeted him as he entered the petrol station shop. He picked a pre-packed turkey and stuffing sandwich from the refrigerator and went to the counter.

"Christmas dinner?" the man behind the checkout asked.

"Jack!" Mervin responded surprised.

Jack Thomas had been working in the post room at the city bank where he had been working himself only a week earlier.

"How's the world of banking?" Jack asked.

"What are you doing working here?" Mervin tried to remember the last time he had seen Jack pushing the post trolley around his department, and he could not, only that it had been awhile.

"I was made redundant last September," Jack told him. "When the going gets tough the tough kick the man at the bottom. Selwyn put in a bad word for me and I was out."

"How long have you been working here?"

"Exactly a week. Three months of looking and this is all I could find. Things could be worse."

"If there's any vacancies going put in a good word for me."

"Et tu Mervin. How's the head?"

"The head?"

"I was in the Thomas Mudd Inn last night. Celebrating my first week of paid employment. You looked a bit worse for wear."

"Did you see someone talking to me?"

"After you left he sat next to me."

Mervin felt relieved that he had not imagined the odd conversation. Ben had acted as though he had not seen anyone.

"Did he ask you anything odd?" Mervin asked.

"Would you rather be shot in the head at first light or burnt next Christmas? That was when I left."

"What was your answer?"

"Bullet between the eyes. Justin Bonner, you don't know him, but he said the man was in there last Christmas Eve. He chose the burning. I'd never seen him before, but he sounds like the local loon."

The roaring sound of an engine turned them both to the window. The nondescript motorcyclist had returned and had stopped by one of the pumps.

"Just the sandwich?" Jack asked.

"And twenty black pack Superkings."

Mervin paid with a credit card and walked back out to the forecourt.

The motorcyclist walked past him heading for the petrol station. Mervin thought he was going to take his helmet off as he reached the door, but he did not.

Mervin stopped and tore the cellophane rapper off the packet of cigarettes and pulled a cigarette out. As he reached into his pocket for his lighter, a loud bang startled him. He turned around expecting to see the motorbike heading away, but the motorcyclist was walking across the forecourt toward the motorbike.

The motorcyclist mounted the motorbike, started the engine and sped away. Mervin looked towards the petrol station shop, but the lighting from the forecourt reflected in the window preventing him from seeing inside. A bad feeling led him to return to the shop, and when he entered he was surprised to find that Jack was nowhere to be seen.

He walked towards the counter and heard a tapping sound. He leaned over and saw Jack lying on the ground, his right leg shaking as though he was having a fit, and then he saw blood pumping from a dark hole between his eyes, which stared straight up, wide and vacant.

He pulled his mobile phone from his jacket pocket and phoned for an ambulance. By the time the call ended, Jack lay still, a pool of blood spreading out around his head.

* * *

"What time did you hear the gun?" a young police detective named Kevin Smith asked Mervin.

Mervin puffed nervously on his third cigarette, ignoring the warning sign attached to the side of the petrol station forbidding smoking on the forecourt.

"First light," Mervin said, and wished that he had not used those words.

"What time was that?"

"I don't know. I left home at about quarter to eight, so sometime between quarter to and half past."

"Could you describe the person that you saw?"

"I didn't see the face. The rider was dressed completely in black and wearing a black helmet with the visor down."

"What type of motorbike was it?"

"I don't know. I didn't pay much attention to the bike."

"Vehicle reg?"

"Won't all this be on the CCTV?"

"If the CCTV had been working it would have been."

"There must be other cameras in the area, even traffic cameras."

"We'll be checking, but in the meantime you shouldn't be leaving town, so if you have any plans for Christmas you'll need to cancel."

"No plans. Just me, a turkey sandwich and a pack of smokes." Mervin felt depressed sharing his plans for Christmas out loud.

* * *

Mervin closed the door and went to the lounge where he turned the radio on and collapsed into an armchair. He lit another cigarette and wondered how many times he would have to listen to Slade wishing everybody a merry Christmas or Wizzard wishing it could be Christmas every day before the end of the day.

He took a deep drag on his cigarette and started choking when he heard the newsreader on the radio mention the name Justin Bonner. By the time he had finished coughing, the news had concluded and Bruce Springsteen was singing "Santa Claus is Comin' To Town."

He sat in the chair for an hour waiting for the news to return, and when it did, the lead story was the shooting at the petrol station. The police were appealing for witnesses. The second story was about a man named Justin Bonner who had suffered horrific burns in an industrial accident at a café in the High Street and had been pronounced dead at the scene. Investigations were to be carried out, but an electrical fault was thought to be the most likely cause.

Mervin wondered whether a nondescript person in black leathers and a black crash helmet had visited the café shortly before or after visiting a petrol station. He found himself trying to remember what the man had looked like that had been sitting next to him at the bar, and found that he could not. He had tried to ignore him in the hope that he would go away, and had been unable to focus clearly when he had tried looking at him. He wondered how long it would take for the police to discover that Jack Thomas and Justin Bonner had known one another.

Mervin stood and fetched a bottle of "Glenmorangie Ealanta" single malt a client had given to him last Christmas. He had been saving it for a special occasion, but suddenly he felt that time might be shorter than he had planned, and the day required not just alcohol, but fine alcohol.

He collapsed back into the armchair and stood the bottle on the floor by his feet. He raised the cigarette to his lips and took several long, slow drags on the filter and watched the smoke drifting away across the room.

He closed his eyes and listened to "Driving Home For Christmas" drifting from the radio, and as he drifted to sleep his mind took him back to the Thomas Mudd Inn. The man was talking to him, and he concentrated on the glass of ale held firmly in his hand.

"Popular choice," the man said. "Justin Bonner screamed out what was left of his lungs and then his blood boiled."

Mervin turned and saw a face lined with age, eyes dark and sunken, lips swollen and red as though ready to burst. The man opened his mouth through a thick black beard to reveal teeth sharpened like daggers.

"Go away," Mervin said too afraid to risk using stronger language.

The mouth formed an ugly smile and the man said: "One year. For you Mervin the clock is ticking."

Mervin opened his eyes and found himself sitting in darkness. The radio was playing "A Fairytale Of New York." Squeezed between his fingers the cigarette had burnt down to the filter and died. On his lap was the unopened pack of turkey sandwiches.

He dropped the filter into an ashtray by the side of the armchair and tore the pack of sandwiches open. He felt famished and ate the sandwich in only a few bites.

He looked about and saw the unopened bottle of whisky standing by his feet. He broke the seal and took a swig. The liquid felt warm as it found its way into his stomach, and the anxiety he had felt on waking slowly faded.

The hourly news came on the radio and the newsreader talked about the shooting. When the newsreader referred to the shooting as having happened yesterday morning Mervin felt as though all of the air had been sucked from his lungs. The next story was about Justin Bonner. Police were now treating the fire as arson and were appealing for witnesses. The fire was yesterday.

Mervin raised his wrist and looked at his watch. It was just past seven and the date was the twenty-sixth. He put the top back on the bottle and got to his feet before confusion dug its claws in too deeply and wobbled as a wave of vertigo passed through him.

He sniffed his shirt and cringed. He had not changed since Christmas Eve, but he felt too anxious for a shower and change. He put the bottle next to the radio and headed for the front door.

* * *

"I didn't see anyone," Ben Mudd said as he looked at Mervin with concern.

Mervin had walked the mile to the Thomas Mudd Inn to set his mind at rest, but the response he had got from Ben had done nothing to alleviate the anxiety.

"The man was sitting right next to me," Mervin told him. "I was drinking and he was just rambling on."

"Why was he talking to you if you don't know him?" Ben asked.

"You *saw* him then?"

"No." Ben looked at his watch as though to say he was too busy to stand around talking. "What I saw was you sitting at the bar drinking, and then you lying on the floor. You were alone and I didn't see anyone talking to you. You had a skinfull. My fault for having kept serving you."

"I didn't imagine it."

"I'm really busy this evening," Ben said.

Mervin turned and started towards the door. Above the door was a CCTV camera. He looked back and saw that the camera would have covered the area where he was sitting.

"What about the cameras?" Mervin called to Ben.

"What *about* the cameras?" Ben asked.

"The man will be on the camera."

"A word of advice Mel . . . Cut down on the ale. Make it a New Year's resolution."

* * *

As the days passed, Mervin made a point of not going to the Thomas Mudd Inn. He was not sure whether he would ever go there again. He was not even sure whether he would drink alcohol ever again. That would be a resolution he would take one day at a time.

Life felt as though it had become stagnant, and he found that although he had not touched a drop of alcohol since Christmas, he was smoking far more than he ever had before. With no income, his savings account was fast drying up, and he refused to claim benefits. Having to wait in a queue at the job centre each week would have felt like an admission of defeat from which there would be no turning back.

By the start of February he was down to his last few pounds, and whatever he did, there would not be enough to cover the rent for the month. Lack of funds had even forced him to stop smoking. He felt that life had finally hit rock bottom when he received a phone call from an old friend named Simon Short. They had been at college together and had both started at the same bank at the start of their careers, but Simon had soon headed across the Atlantic to the riches of New York.

Simon had started his own asset management company, and he was looking for someone he could trust to head up an office in London, and Mervin had been the first person he had thought of. A meeting in London was arranged, and within weeks, his life shifted from neutral to first, and by May he was earning more money in a month than he had earned in an entire year before his fall.

By June he felt confident enough to ask his personal assistant Jenny Brown out on a date, and by August they were engaged to be married.

During September they moved into their new home; a seven bedroom Elizabethan manor on a wooded hill overlooking the picturesque town of Westerham, 23 miles to the southeast of London. The grounds had a boating lake, tennis courts, swimming pool and, even though neither of them had plans to take up the game, a croquet lawn.

The year raced by, and as Christmas approached Mervin found himself feeling anxious. At first he could not understand what was making him feel worried, and then at the start of December he started having nightmares. At night he found himself sitting back at the bar in the Thomas Mudd Inn nursing a pint of ale while the voice of a man he could not quite remember echoed around the inside of his head like a pinball. Each time he turned to look at the face of his tormentor, he woke and spent what was left of the night staring at the ceiling trying to steady his nerves.

On Christmas Eve, Mervin left his office at five and took a black cab north to Walthamstow. He walked to the Thomas Mudd Inn and just stood staring at the façade wondering why he had come back to the place that was the cause of his nightmares. It was Christmas Eve and Jenny was waiting for him to get home. The Thomas Mudd Inn was part of his old life, and a lot had changed since then. He wanted to turn and walk away, but instead he pushed the door open and walked into the bar.

There were more people inside than he had been expecting, but nothing much had changed. It looked just as he remembered it. He looked around, but did not recognize anyone. He supposed life moved on quickly in a large city.

He walked to the bar but did not recognize the man pulling pints for a group at the far end of the bar. He sat at a stool and realized that he was sitting in exactly the same place he had been sitting in exactly twelve months earlier.

He sat staring down at the bar trying to remember. A pint of ale appeared in front of him and he looked up to see the barman standing in front of him.

"I didn't order anything," Mervin told him.

"He . . ." the barman started as he looked to his left. "He's gone."

"Who's gone?" Mervin asked feeling awkward.

"I was just talking to a man and he bought you a pint of Blackhorse Ale. Said he was an old acquaintance and you always drink Blackhorse Ale."

"What did he look like?"

"He was . . ." The barman stopped again, and then said, "I only spoke to him no more than a couple of minutes ago, and I'll be damned if I can't remember."

"What happened to Ben Mudd?"

"Ben Mudd?"

"I used to live around here. He was the landlord. I haven't been in her since last Christmas Eve."

"He was killed. Terrible. My brother knew him. There were a couple of murders last Christmas. Both the victims had been in here the night before they were killed. He was on his way to see the police with the CCTV footage when he was killed. A camera covers the bar. Run down by the station. Someone saw a motorcyclist racing away, but no one was ever caught. Probably never will be."

"I didn't know."

"No rest for the wicked," the barman said and headed back down to the other end of the bar to serve another group of drinkers.

Mervin picked the glass up and stared at the brown liquid. He had not touched a drop of alcohol for twelve months, but the smell of the ale brought on a craving he thought he had beaten forever. He raised the glass to his lips, took a small sip and returned it to the bar.

"That's all it takes."

Mervin turned to see who had spoken to him, but there was no one there. He looked around the bar, but no one was paying him any attention. He looked at his watch and suddenly felt very guilty about not going straight home. Jenny would be wondering where he was. He had switched his mobile off, but she would probably phone his office and someone would tell her that he had left over an hour ago and she would start worrying.

He stood refusing to look at the pint of ale for a moment longer. His old life was in the past and that was the best place for it. His new life was where he wanted to be, and it was waiting for him on the other side of the city.

He looked up at the camera above the door as he left and wondered what it was that Ben Mudd had seen that had made him decide to take the footage to the police. He wondered whether the motorbike that had prevented him from reaching the police was black and being ridden by a nondescript rider clad in black leathers with a black helmet, face concealed behind a heavily tinted visor.

The temperature had dropped while he had been sitting in the Thomas Mudd Inn and an icy breeze stung his face. A black cab was approaching along the road, so he stepped up to the curb and raised his hand. It pulled up next to him and he got in.

* * *

The cab headed south on the A12 towards the Blackwall Tunnel. There was more traffic on the road than he thought there would be, but he supposed people were heading out of the city for Christmas.

The skyscrapers of Canary Wharf loomed up on his right and then the queue for the tunnel started. The only words the driver had spoken since he had got into the cab was "Where to?" at the start, and Mervin was glad. He did not feel like conversation. All he wanted to do was get home.

He switched his mobile phone on and saw that there was no signal. The time was half past six. He wondered what time first light was on Christmas Day. He remembered leaving home at a quarter to eight the previous Christmas Day, so first light would be about 13 hours away. He pushed the thought away. Within the hour he would be tucked up in bed in the safety of his perfect home with his perfect wife, and it would be the best Christmas either of them had ever experienced. He would make sure of it.

The traffic in front started moving and the cab followed down the slope and into the mouth of the tunnel. Mervin jumped as a huge road tanker thundered past, the sound of the diesel engine reverberating off the walls and the 10 wheels pushing down on the tarmac.

The trailer was painted silver with the words Navitas Petroleum in red along its side.

Popular choice.

Mervin shivered. The fact that it was at least 13 hours until first light did nothing to allay the anxiety that was building.

Mervin felt a deep sense of relief as the cab emerged into the night of south-east London and quickly left the tunnel behind. The traffic was moving freely, and by his reckoning he would be home by 7:30.

As they drove down the slip road and joined the M25 motorway, snow started falling. At first the fall was light, but enough for most drivers to slow causing all those following to brake. As the snow got heavier, the traffic came to a standstill and the snow settled across the surface of the motorway.

"Why has everyone stopped?" Mervin said to himself. "It's only snow."

"Human nature," the cab driver said.

"How many miles is it to Westerham?"

"Ten miles."

"It would be quicker to walk."

"I'm sure that is what Oates thought."

"Sorry?" Mervin said thrown by the comment.

"Terra Nova 1912. I may be gone for some time."

"I wouldn't have plans to come back here."

"A good traveler has no fixed pans, and is not intent on arriving."

Mervin resisted the urge to ask what he was talking about and looked at his watch. It was a quarter to seven. He did not want to be sitting in the back of a cab on the motorway all night, and he was sure that he could walk 10 miles in no more than three to four hours.

He switched his mobile phone on and it beeped at him. The message was from Jenny and it said: 'Where are you? Call me.'

He was about to phone, but instead just pressed the reply. He did not want to face a hundred questions about how he ended up stuck in the snow on the motorway. He typed "Stuck in snow. Going to walk. Home by 11." He pressed send and prayed that he would be home by 11 thinking midnight would have been more optimistic.

"How much do I owe you?" Mervin asked.

"Ordinarily the journey would have been four score, but then ordinarily I would not have found myself sitting in the snow for all eternity."

Mervin pulled his wallet from his pocket and opened it to see what notes he had. He took out four 50's and leant forward to pass them to the cab driver. A hand raised and took the notes from him without looking back. Mervin caught a brief glimpse of the cab driver's eyes in the rear view mirror and felt cold. The moment had been short, but the dark eyes that stared back at him left him cold.

"Ten score should . . ." He stopped himself, and said, "Two hundred pounds should cover it."

"The wages of a hired man are not to remain with you all night until morning."

Mervin opened the door and stepped out into the cold. If he had realized just how cold it would be outside the cab, he might have had second thoughts about trying to walk, but he had paid the fare, and as soon as he slammed the door closed, he felt a sense of relief to be leaving the cab driver, his strange comments and those unsettling dark eyes behind.

He looked back. Three lanes of cars disappeared into a swirling fog of snow, an icy cold wind blowing snow from the surrounding fields. He turned and looked in the direction he would be walking, and he could see no further than about four cars. He buttoned up his coat, pushed his hands into his pockets and started walking.

* * *

Mervin felt as though he had been walking for hours, but he refused to look at his watch through fear of seeing just how little time had passed. Snow had settled on the windscreens of the cars and stuck to the windows along their sides, and no other person had left the relative warmth of their cars. He could not see anyone and, even though he knew there must be hundreds of stranded people around him, he felt as though he was completely alone.

He continued on, one foot in front of the other. He passed a large signpost, but the writing was covered with a layer of snow blasted to its surface by the wind. His face felt numb. His fingers hurt, the cold getting to the tips even through the fabric of his pockets. A pain was building in his toes and he wondered how cold it had to be and how long it took to develop frostbite.

He had driven along the motorway many times, but he had never strayed from its path. There had never been any reason to, but he was sure that towns and villages could not be far from it. Nowhere in the overcrowded southeast was far from some form of habitation.

He stopped and looked towards the steep bank that led up from the hard shoulder. If there was a town at the top, he was sure that he could find someone with a four wheel drive vehicle that could be persuaded to drive him cross country back to Westerham.

He turned and headed for the bank. Without stopping he started up the slope. It was steep and he had to take his hands out of his pockets to keep himself from falling.

As he reached the top a blast of wind almost threw him back down, but he somehow managed to stand his ground. The snow felt like grit against his face and the cold air was smothering, but he was determined not to give up. He doubted whether he would ever be able to find the cab again even if he did turn back.

Through squinted eyes he looked about, but the waves of snow blasting him made visibility beyond a few yards impossible. He was sure that there must be houses only a stone's throw from where he was standing. Developers had stuck housing estates all over the countryside.

He pushed on, his legs sinking into the snow up to his knees. He wondered whether anyone would find him before he froze to death if he fell and broke his leg. He doubted it. He would have to crawl back to the motorway assuming he did not get lost in the maelstrom of snowflakes and end up crawling around in circles until his muscles gave way and the snow covered his dying body.

He walked in a straight line, or as straight a line as he could with nothing to guide his way, hoping that by doing so he would at least stumble upon a road, assuming he could distinguish a country road covered in snow from the surrounding countryside covered in snow.

A dark shape appeared ahead, and as he neared he saw that it was a house. He started walking quicker and his right ankle twisted painfully in a hole beneath the snow and he fell onto his side where he lay hoping he had not done any serious damage.

As the pain subsided and became an uncomfortable throb, he got back onto his feet, cringing as he put weight onto his right foot. He guessed it was sprained, but he had no choice but to walk on it.

The house looked substantial, and around it were old wooden barns. He could not see whether there were any lights on in the house or not through the snow, but he assumed there must be someone home.

He slowly made his way towards the house following what looked like hoofed animal prints in the snow. He could not tell what type of animal had made the prints, or whether they followed the path of a driveway or grass. He only hoped that his good ankle did not find another hole. He did not think he would make it even to the house with two damaged ankles.

* * *

He knocked on the door and it moved. He pushed and the door swung back to reveal a dark entrance hall. Through the gloom he could see that strips of wallpaper had fallen from the walls. Wires dangled from a hole in the ceiling where a light had once been fitted and the floor was littered with empty tins and bottles.

"Is anyone in there?" he called.

He was not certain whether he would feel safer if someone called back or not. At least that way he would know. Silence would create an uncomfortable feeling that someone was watching him from the shadows.

He walked across the threshold and stood in the center of the entrance hall. A rush of cold air made him shiver and the front door slammed closed. He assumed there was a through draft, but the slamming door had already done its work on his nerves.

When he tried the door it would not open. He tried pulling the catch back on the lock, but the door would still not open. He turned and walked through an opening into what he assumed was once the sitting room.

The floor was wooden, and from its poor state he guessed that it had once been carpeted. A large stone fireplace occupied the center of the far wall. All traces of the people that had once lived in the house had been removed, and he doubted that the house would ever be lived in again.

He hobbled back out to the hall and looked up the stairs. He made his way up, his ankle only making a mild protest, and found that the doors to the rooms—he counted four—had been removed.

He hobbled into the room to his right and went to the window and looked out. The wind howled as it passed and, if anything, the storm seemed to be getting worse.

He slumped to the floor with his back against the wall. He tried phoning Jenny, but he could not get a signal. He did not know whether it was the location or just the storm that prevented him making the call, but he did know that Jenny would soon be becoming very anxious about his whereabouts.

He raised his wrist to check the time, but his watch had stopped, the second hand frozen over the seven. The battery was only a few weeks old, so he assumed it had been knocked a little too hard when he had fallen.

He closed his eyes and listened to the wind blowing the snow against the windows. The sound undulated and, as his breathing steadied, he felt his anxieties draining away.

* * *

Mervin stared at Ben Mudd as he spoke. He was not interested in listening. He stood and walked towards the door. Sitting at a table by the door was Jack Thomas and someone he knew to be Justin Bonner. They both looked up and smiled at him. He knew they had both been talking about him the way people do. He felt nothing but hate toward them.

He found himself standing in the petrol station. Jack looked up and he raised his hand. He held a gun and when Jack opened his mouth to say something he pulled the trigger and a hole appeared between his eyes as the wall behind turned red.

He was standing outside a Victorian semi-detached house. The door opened and he slammed the sole of his right shoe into a man's stomach sending him to the ground. He poured petrol over the man. The smell of the liquid was almost overpowering. He lit a match and dropped it onto the man. There was a flash of light and he turned away.

He saw a small black circle and then a gun came into focus. A black gloved hand held the gun, but beyond that his eyes refused to focus on the face.

"Between the eyes," a voice that seemed vaguely familiar said. "Popular choice."

"I chose fire," Mervin said with the same irritation he reserved for waiters when they brought him the wrong order.

"Never say fire to a man with a loaded gun."

"Who are you?" Mervin asked, his eyes refusing to focus on the face.

"Call me father time. All I have is time and my games to while away that time."

"Are you going to kill me?" Mervin asked surprised at the calmness in his voice.

"I really would like to tell you that I'm here to spread the joys of Christmas, but that would be a lie. Whatever I am, I am not a liar."

"Why?" Mervin asked. "If you're going to murder me, at least tell me why?"

"How old does a man have to be before he grows tired of life? That depends upon the man I suppose. There you were at the bottom looking up, and now you're looking down. You have a beautiful wife, a beautiful house and in nine month's time a beautiful son . . ."

"Jenny isn't pregnant," Mervin said, his skin prickling as though something tiny was scuttling about beneath his clothes.

"A son you will never know, and who will never know you."

"Why are you doing this to me?" Mervin shouted.

"You did this to yourself," the man told him. "You went in search of the past and you walked here of your own free will, and now you sit here alone in the dark with nothing but your past to hold you together."

Mervin tried to stand, but his ankle had swollen and gave. He slumped back to the ground gritting his teeth tightly against the stabbing pain. His face felt hot and his heart was pounding. He closed his eyes tightly and waited for the pain to subside, and eventually it settled down to a dull but bearable throb.

He opened his eyes and the man was gone. He looked about the room, but he was alone. He looked down and saw a handgun lying on the floor by his feet. He reached out and stopped just short, his fingers hovering over the handgun as though afraid to touch it.

He lowered his hand and touched the handle, surprised that it felt warm as though someone had very recently had it clutched tightly in their hand. He had thought the man had been nothing but his imagination, but the handgun brought him into reality.

He was about to call out, but stopped himself. He did not want to see the man again. He wondered whether the gun had been left for him to shoot himself with. He wondered whether the man was waiting to see what he would do. He wondered whether it was the same gun that had shot Jack Thomas in the head.

He picked the handgun up allowing his fingers to curl around the handle and his forefinger to pass through the trigger guard and rest against the trigger.

"What do you expect me to do?" he asked, not expecting an answer. "Shoot myself?"

He sat still, his breathing slow and steady, listening for any sort of response, but all he could hear was the wind howling around the outside of the house.

With his free hand he pulled his mobile phone from his pocket and pressed the small button below the screen. The display lit up and he was surprised to see that he had a full signal. He saw the time and froze. It was six thirty.

He had checked the time as he had left the tunnel back at Blackwall, and it had been a quarter to seven. He could not understand how it could possibly only be six thirty.

He touched the BBC icon on the screen and a small clock appeared. The air felt as though it had frozen in his lungs. It *was* six thirty, but the date was the twenty-fifth. He realized he must have fallen asleep and now it was almost dawn.

He thought of the man that had been standing in the room tormenting him, and assumed it had been a dream. He looked at the handgun he held in his right hand. The handgun was definitely real. A nauseating sensation was creeping up from his stomach. He had to phone Jenny and let her know that he was alright.

There were three messages on the phone, two from Jenny and one from an unknown number. He considered ignoring the messages and phoning Jenny, but he felt that knowing whether she was worried or just angry would prepare him.

Forewarned is forearmed, he thought and listened to the first message: "I thought you said you'd be home by 11:00. Where are you? Call me."

Not too worried, Melvin thought. *Slightly annoyed maybe.*

He listened to the second message: "Where are you? The police are here. What happened? Wherever you are just phone me."

Mervin stared at the phone taken aback by the last message. Why had she called the police? He could not understand why the police had gone to the house. He was sure they must receive hundreds of calls every week about people not arriving home when they were supposed to. They would never get anything done if they ran after every report.

He listened to the third message expecting to hear Jenny, but instead it was a man's voice: "My name is Detective Inspector David North. Please phone me on 077 9060 2543."

Mervin felt his skin crawling. He was late getting home. He knew he was *very* late, and he had not got home, but a detective inspector seemed a bit over the top.

He returned to the BBC website and scrolled down. The top story was titled "M25 Murder Hunt." He tapped the line and the story appeared.

A cab driver was brutally murdered in his cab on the M25 on Christmas Eve. Traffic was brought to a standstill in both directions by heavy snowfall. The body of Frederic Baker was discovered by police checking on vehicles stranded by the snow. CCTV recorded a man believed to be Mervin Shaldon from Kent getting into the cab in Walthamstow in East London. Police have said that Mervin Shaldon is wanted for questioning, and they have said that he should not be approached. He is believed to be armed and dangerous. Anyone with any information should contact . . . .

Mervin felt cold. The article had not said how the cab driver had been killed, only that he had been *brutally murdered*. He looked at the handgun and felt that he knew how the cab driver had been killed. He wanted to phone the detective inspector, but he was holding the murder weapon and he was sure the man that had left it on the floor for him to pick up had not left any prints on it. He was also sure that the same gun would be found to be linked to a murder at an east London petrol station exactly twelve months ago.

At least I'm not burning, Melvin thought, but felt little comfort from the thought.

He shuffled his bottom across the floor to the window. He placed his mobile phone and the handgun on the sill and pulled himself up putting all his weight onto his good ankle. He looked through the window at a snow covered field. In the distance he could see lights from a built up area. He could not tell whether it was a town or just a cluster of houses, but there would be a phone, and he needed to phone his lawyer.

He was sure that the moment the detective inspector knew where he was there would be a team of armed police speeding towards him, none full of the joys of Christmas, all wanting to get the job done and return to their tinsel decked station.

His lawyer was Max Westengburg, and although he was a corporate lawyer, he would be able to bring some control and order to the situation. He knew he would not get far with his twisted ankle, and there was no point trying to lose the gun when the area would be carefully searched by an army of police officers. An enthusiastic young constable eager to impress fishing the murder weapon from a ditch or bush would make him look more guilty than if he just handed it to the police. He had done nothing wrong, so he had nothing to hide. He did not believe it would be that simple, but he was out of options.

Slowly he transferred his weight onto his other ankle, his muscles tensing ready for the pain that he knew would follow. There was a dull ache, almost a numbness, but it was bearable. He knew that walking across the deep snow would be a different proposition altogether, but if he was careful, he knew he could make it.

The snow was no longer falling, but the wind was whipping waves of snow up from the ground and spinning it around like mini cyclones across the field. To the west the sky was getting lighter, thinning clouds painted like dark streaks across a grey canvas.

He made his way to the top of the stairs and looked down. He had never imagined something as simple as walking down a flight of stairs would ever seem like such an obstacle.

He hopped down the first three steps, wincing with every jolt, and sat deciding it would be easier to work his way down on his bottom. It felt very undignified, but he did not care. He held the mobile phone in his left hand and the handgun in his right, and he felt so tense he was worried that if the phone rang, he would accidentally answer with the gun and put a bullet in his brain.

Is there a bullet in the gun?

It had not occurred to him to check to see whether the gun was even loaded. He knew nothing about guns. He had never held a handgun before. Apart from television, he had never even seen a real handgun before, although he knew it was a revolver from the cylinder and it looked like a very old revolver.

He did not expect the front door to open without a struggle, but it opened without so much as a squeak. He stepped out shivering as the icy cold wind surrounded him and he was suddenly blinded by a bright light. He instinctively raised his right hand to shield his eyes and a voice boomed at him: "Put the gun down and put your hands on your head."

Mervin lowered the gun and squinted his eyes. There were police standing about a hundred yards away. He could not count how many there were, but he could see that they were armed, and he guessed they considered him to be armed and dangerous.

Without thinking he stepped backwards into the house and closed the door. He expected the phone to ring, and when it did not, he could not think of any reasons why they would try phoning him. The house was empty. They would be able to take him out any time they wanted.

He turned and nearly fell. The walls had been damp with strips of wallpaper peeling away, but now there was no trace of decay. He looked down and saw that the floor was carpeted.

He hobbled through the doorway into the sitting room. A fire smoldered in the large stone fireplace, a man and a woman sat on a large sofa, their mouths wide open as though caught by surprise, blood streaked down their faces from bullet holes in their foreheads; one each between the eyes.

The voice boomed at him from outside: "Come out with your hands raised above your head."

He felt as though he was going mad. When he had entered the house it had been in the slow process of decay. The house had been empty. He tried telling himself that he was dreaming. He bit his tongue and felt pain.

He walked across the room and stopped in front of the man and woman on the sofa. Their eyes stared at him, glazed and frozen at the moment of death. The expression engraved on their faces was not surprise, but terror. The expressions of people given just enough time to know that they are about to die.

Mervin frowned as he realized that he recognized the man. The last time he had seen the face was as he had walked him to the door and shown him out onto the pavement on his last day at the bank. His name was Robert Selwyn and he had been his manager. The man he had blamed at the time for pushing him out and introducing him to the depressing world of unemployment. He had only met his wife once. That had been at the company's Christmas party, and he remembered the face.

He raised his phone and scrolled down to "Jenny." He phoned and the call connected immediately. Before she could say anything, Mervin said, "I didn't do it."

A man responded: "Leave the gun in the house and walk out the front door with your hands raised above your head."

"Are you Detective Inspector David North?" Mervin asked.

"Yes." There was a brief pause, and then he continued: "Can I talk to Robert Selwyn?"

Mervin did not know how to respond, and then asked, "Can I talk to Jenny?"

There was another pause, this time longer, and then he heard Jenny's voice: "Why?" she asked. "Why did you do it?"

"Someone set me up," Mervin responded, but he did not know what he could do to prove it. If even Jenny thought that he was guilty, he had no chance of persuading Detective Inspector David North and his team of officers directing their firepower at the house.

"They spoke to the landlord of a pub in Walthamstow and he said you were there last night. When you left you left a videotape behind. It showed you talking to two men last Christmas Eve. You said you were going to kill them both."

"There's no audio on CCTV," Mervin said, and wished that he had not said anything.

"The police have people that can lip read. Why did you do it?"

Mervin ended the call. He had no memory of talking to anyone other than the man that started the nightmare and Ben Mudd, but he also had no memory of getting home.

"I didn't do it," Mervin said to himself. "I've never owned a gun."

He thought back to the petrol station. He had not been drunk when he had walked into the petrol station, and he remembered the conversation with Jack Thomas. He did not even know Justin Bonner let alone where he lived.

He wondered whether the man that had done such a spectacular job of destroying his life was watching the house waiting to see how his game played out. He was sure that he would be, but he could not help but feel a deep and sickening sense of confusion. How had the man got to the cab driver? He supposed he could have been following, but he could not understand how he could possibly have predicted the snow storm bringing the traffic to a standstill, and his wandering away from the motorway and stumbling upon the house of Robert Selwyn.

He closed his eyes and tried to remember back twelve months. A pain started building between his eyes, intensifying with every passing second. He saw Jack Thomas standing behind the counter in the petrol station. His mouth was opening and closing, but he could not hear the words. A hole appeared between his eyes and, for a moment, he stood, his mouth stuck open, then dark blood poured down his face and he collapsed out of sight.

He opened his eyes and realized that he was shaking. He was going to be sent to prison for the rest of his life and he could not see any way to avoid it. All he had was a hazy memory of a man in a pub he would not be able to describe. The only way to avoid prison would be a high security psychiatric hospital.

Heart beating fiercely in his chest, he raised the gun and pointed the nozzle into his mouth. His forefinger tensed against the trigger. One way or another his life was over, but if he pulled the trigger he was accepting defeat. Everyone would see it as an admission of guilt. He lowered the gun and decided he was going to clear his name. Out of all the wrongs of the world, the one thing he always believed was that, whatever happens in life, eventually the truth always outs.

He walked towards the doorway back out to the front door and kicked something on the floor. It fell over making a dull metallic sound. He looked down and saw a large green jerry can. The cap was missing and the smell of petrol filled his senses.

He looked at his clothes and saw that they were soaked in petrol. The smell attacked his senses and he gagged. He hobbled out to the front door and opened it and started towards the light still directed at him.

The voice boomed once more: "Put the gun down."

Melvin tossed the gun away and continued forward and, through his streaming eyes, he saw three people approaching.

"Don't shoot," Mervin shouted.

The three men reached him and he stopped. He raised his hand and rubbed his eyes to clear the tears that had formed and saw one of the officers pointing something at him. He thought it was a handgun, and then time seemed to slow as he saw two small metal darts launch towards him, fine wires trailing back to a Taser.

Mervin tried to move out of the way, but not quickly enough. The glow of the sun appeared on the horizon and fifty thousand volts coursed through his body, his petrol soaked clothes igniting. He fell to his knees as his muscles contracted uncontrollably and, as his burning clothes stuck to his body, he looked up and saw the face of the tormentor looking down at him and smiling through pointed teeth and a tangled black beard, eyes glowing points of red and horns twisting into smoke.

The pain was intense, and he knew he was going to die. He knew he was going to die condemned in the minds of all who knew him.

* * *

One Year Later

Jenny reached the end of the driveway and saw that the gatehouse was occupied. It had been one of Mervin's plans to renovate the old Victorian building and rent it out to rich holidaymakers from the city. When he had died, she had sold the building to raise some quick money.

Samuel was three months old, and she was determined that he would never go without anything. She kept wondering how Christmas could have been if Mervin had still been alive. Samuel would never know his father, but she refused to let the terrible events of the previous Christmas drag her down.

A black motorbike stood on its side stand in the small garden at the front of the property. There were no signs of Christmas, not even a wreath attached to the front door. The windows were rectangles of darkness, and the longer she stared, the worse she felt. She had once been told a story about a being called Krampus, and she had suffered nightmares for several weeks following. He was Santa's evil twin. She had stopped believing in Santa long ago, but the sense of ill will that radiated from the darkness within brought back memories of those dreams, and they made her shiver.

When she returned home, she phoned Theresa Simmons the local estate agent. She felt an almost overwhelming sense of dread, and she did not think the feeling would leave all the while she stayed close to the gatehouse and its new occupant.

That night she dreamt she was sitting alone in a bar when an old man sat next to her and asked what felt like a strange question. When she awoke, it was still dark outside, and she could not remember the answer she had given any more than she could remember any detail of the man's face, but the voice of the old man stayed with her like an echo: "*Popular choice.*"

* * *

Guy Burtenshaw lives in a small town in southern England and has been writing horror stories for many years. He has self-published several horror novels and his short stories can be found in various magazines and anthologies. He also writes murder mystery novels under the pseudonym G D Shaw.

The Ninth Night of Krampus

NOTHING TO DREAD
by Jeff Provine

Inspiration: Jeff writes: "While researching Krampus, I was struck how it was an incorporation of an older religious spirit filling the need to punish bad little boys and girls while St. Nick rewarded the good ones. Without consequences, kids run wild. I wanted to do a story from the beginning where a kid fought back in an attempt to be a good boy, but it would ultimately mean backfiring." Or does it backfire? You decide, Dear Reader.

His cloven hooves made stalwart clacks against the cobblestone street. Rusty chains sat on his shoulders, wrapped carefully over the matted brown fur so they rattled with every step. In his clawed hands, he carried the bundle of birch twigs still warm from the backsides of children farther down the street.

All around him, the town was quiet. Doors were locked. Windows were latched tight with the curtains drawn behind them. There were few lights and even fewer whispers. Somewhere behind him, he could hear a bad child whimpering. At least now he knew to keep his crying soft enough not to disturb his parents. Krampus prowled tonight, and it wouldn't be beyond him to make a second trip.

He stopped at the three-story house in the middle of the street. Its white face had been recently repainted with a pastoral scene between the wooden beams. He sniffed the cold air with his hircine nostrils.

The parents were good folk, avoiding the pitfalls of wealth with generosity and kindness. The girl, Anna, was good, too. She did her chores with a contented smile. She helped her mother without being asked. She had even given her doll to the poor girl who was sick two streets over, where Krampus had whipped the boy who stole from the larder to stuff his gluttonous face. The warm spice of Anna's goodness burned Krampus's nose.

He turned away from it to the sickly sweet stench of badness that came from the boy, Jakob. Krampus had never visited the boy before, but Jakob was 10 now, that age when boys begin to think of the trouble they can cause. In the past month alone, this boy had been caught loitering in the church when he should have been doing chores. Then he began playing with his father's hunting traps. The worst was his stealing from rich old Herr Eckles, who had taken up newfangled photography, that mad art that trapped a piece of the unwitting human's soul in a portrait.

Krampus snorted and mumbled to himself in his gruff voice, "Photography. What fools humans are."

He stamped his hoof in front of the house. The front door began to groan.

He stamped again. Its locks ticked as the bolts slid free.

He stamped a third time, and the door opened wide with a loud, slow, long creak.

Krampus felt his furred neck bristle. He tightened his grip on the birch switches and heard them screech together.

The house was dark, but his ancient eyes had no problem piercing the darkness. His pointed ears made out the sounds of the snoring parents and the soft sleeping breaths of Anna. They would sleep through the whole of Jakob's lesson thanks to the Krampus's power.

Jakob was still awake. He could hear the fast beating of the boy's heart. Krampus felt his lip pull back enough in a smile to let the cold air sting some of his sharp teeth.

He strode into the house, careful not to touch the power of the threshold, and set a hoof quietly onto the floorboards. They whined under his evil touch.

His hooves crossed the boards and the rugs, leaving small rings of ash as prints. Krampus stalked up the stairs, pressing his weight on them one by one to make them squeal. Jakob's heart pounded louder and louder.

In the upstairs hall, the smells of Anna mixed with the odor of Jakob's bad deeds. Krampus spat and hurried past Anna's room. Nicholas and the Christ child would visit her soon enough. He had more important work to do than bribing children for saying "yes, please" and "thank you." Krampus was here to punish the wicked.

He stopped in front of Jakob's door and raised his clawed hand to the wood. First he scratched, louder and louder until he raked his claws to the doorknob. Then he opened the door and leaned inside.

A horrid flash, ten times the brightness of lightning, exploded in the room. Krampus screamed and dropped his birch sticks. He stabbed his claws into his eyes to drown out the pain.

Then there was a clap, not of thunder, but the sharp shriek of iron. More pain bit deep into Krampus's leg halfway up from the hoof. He let out a howl that roared like a bear and bleated like a goat. Krampus could feel his Hell-warmed blood trickling down his leg.

Krampus tugged at his leg against a heavy weight. He blinked his square eyes until they could see in the dark again. It was iron, a sharp-toothed trap meant for wolves.

A match lit up in the shadows, and a lantern began its warm glow on the bedside table. From under the blankets, Jakob's voice sang, "*Wundervoll!*"

Krampus growled back at him. "Release me!"

Jakob pushed back the blankets. He was still fully dressed in his leather pants and coat. "No, Herr Krampus, I will not be doing a thing like that."

Krampus tugged again at his leg. The trap was linked to a stake in the floor by a chain.

It wasn't the only trap on the floor. They were laid out in a three-tiered circle completely around the doorway. No matter where Krampus had stumbled in his blindness, he was bound to be caught.

Above the door, a wire ran to a smoldering plate of camera flash powder, ignited when the door had opened. Another wire ran from the windowpane.

Jakob stepped out of bed and expertly glided his little boots between them. Krampus stared down at him, almost twice his height.

"Release me, boy!" Krampus commanded.

Jakob looked up at him with wide blue eyes. "I know you're my elder, Herr Krampus, but I'm going to disobey."

Krampus grunted. "That is one more lashing you'll get from me."

He patted his belt for his switch, but it wasn't there. Snorting with surprise, he searched for his lost *ruten*. It rested in the hall, where he had dropped it in the flash.

The boy ducked beneath his reach out into the hall and picked up the bundle of birch.

Jakob narrowed his eyes. They shone like blue sparks. "You won't be lashing anyone ever again."

He broke off one of the twigs with his little hands.

Krampus gasped. "How dare you, you miserable mortal doomed to die!"

"Die and go to Heaven." Jakob stuck out his tongue. "You burn in Hell all but one night a year, and then on Judgment Day, what'll happen to you?"

Krampus growled deep in his throat. He did not like to think about the Lake of Fire. His furry coat bristled as he shuddered inside it.

The little boy turned and walked away.

Krampus lunged after him. The iron trap held tight to his leg and stopped him, the boy's blonde hair just inches beyond the Krampus's outstretched claw.

Krampus pulled back his claws and leaned over the trap. He carefully knitted his fingers between the teeth and tried to pry it open. His muscles strained and he groaned, but the trap would not budge. He fell back, panting the cold night air. In the flickering light, he saw crude letters etched into the trap spelling out the name of God over and over.

He snorted. The boy was smart, but being smart was as dangerous as being rich. Krampus felt his lips pull back into a smile. He called after Jakob, "Never mind me, you should worry about yourself. Heaven is for good boys, not boys visited by Krampus for being bad."

The little white face appeared out of the darkness. Krampus almost shrank back in horror before he stopped himself.

"Don't you do that," Jakob warned.

Krampus made his voice as sweet as poisoned honey. "Do what? I'm just trying to point out a fact. If you really want to be good, you might start by releasing a poor creature caught in a painful trap." He whined and made his chains rattle.

Jakob's blue eyes were cold. His hands were behind his back.

"Think of how Saint Peter would look at such generosity. Don't you want to be a good little boy?"

Jakob shook his head slowly.

Krampus blinked. His chains rustled.

"I'm tired of being just good," Jakob said softly. "I want to be great. I want to do something that will make an impact for generations."

Krampus shifted backward. "What do you mean to do, boy?"

Jakob pulled his hands out from behind his back, revealing the huge family Bible, bound in leather hundreds of years before.

Krampus hissed at it and shielded his eyes.

"Herr Krampus," Jakob said, his voice firm and serious, "starting immediately, you will leave my house and never return. Tonight is the last night you will come into my town."

A laugh welled up inside the Krampus. It wasn't the high-pitched chatter he made when a bad child's cried, it was a deep and true laugh that sprang out of him, braying and spitting. It was the first laugh he had given in a long time.

"You don't have the power to do that! Who do you think you are? Solomon? The Archangel Michael?"

"No. I don't have that kind of power."

Krampus wiped a tear from his eye, stinking like sulfur. "Obviously you don't."

"It'll be your promise. And we both know that a demon must keep an oath when he makes it. Only humans are able to go back on our fallible words."

Krampus almost laughed again. "Oh? You're so clever aren't you? You may be smart, boy, even smart enough to trap me, but how could you make me take a vow?"

"It's late, but I can't seem to fall asleep. I think I'll do some reading."

The boy carefully placed the Bible on the floor and sat down next to it. Krampus suddenly felt his stomach, light with laughter, grow heavy.

Jakob peeked up with an arched eyebrow. "Vow that you'll never return to Leonding, and I'll let you go."

Krampus growled. He tugged at the trap again, but it only bit deeper into his leg.

"I believe I'll start with some Psalms," Jakob said. He turned to the middle of the massive tome and traced the lines with his finger. "Blessed is the man who walketh not in the counsel of the ungodly, nor standeth . . ."

Each syllable stung Krampus's ears like a hornet again and again. He tried to dig his claws in deep to drown out the sounds and pressed his eyes closed, but nothing seemed to stop the holy words. He stamped his free hoof and doubled over.

The pain was unbearable, but he could not lose to a child, a *bad* child! They were his domain. He should have been the one to cause the pain. He should have whipped Jakob so he couldn't sit until the New

Year. He should have stuffed Jakob into his tub and carted him away to burn with him. Jakob should have felt this agony!

Krampus lasted until the twenty-third Psalm, when he collapsed to the floor under the words "green pastures."

"Enough!" he roared.

Jakob paused. "You promise?"

"I promise!" Krampus howled. "I will leave and never visit this forsaken town ever again!"

Jakob closed the Bible. Without a word, he stood and got a broom. Using it as a pry, he opened the mouth of the trap.

Krampus pulled his hoof free and shuffled across the floor away from the boy. He nearly bumped into the Bible and fled from it as well. When he bumped into the wall, he clawed his way up to stand, leaving marks in the plaster.

Jakob took a step toward Krampus, brandishing his own birch sticks like a club. "Now leave and never come back."

Krampus limped to the hall window. Tears and snot and blood poured down his face. He spoke with words broken by sobs.

"See how you like it, living in a world where bad little boys aren't punished!"

Jakob smiled. "We have our consciences."

Krampus growled and shoved the window open. He jumped out into the cold night.

In the darkness, he hung in the air. He could not fall; his hooves were banished from touching the cobblestone street below. Forces even more powerful than he kept him to his word. Not even gravity could break a demon's oath. The wind blew him toward Vienna.

There would be no punishment for Nina who pulled her sister's hair or Adolf who refused to study. Jakob's town was forever freed of the Krampus.

* * *

Jeff Provine is a farm kid turned composition professor. He draws web comics, blogs Alternate History, and writes freelance. The summer of 2014 saw the publication of his steampunk Celestial Voyages series and a YA genre-bender Dawn on the Infinity. Learn more about Jeff at www.jeffprovine.com.

The Tenth Night of Krampus:

RAW RECRUITS

by Mark Mills

Inspiration: Mark writes, "Growing up in an area with a strong Germanic heritage, I can't even remember the first time I heard about Krampus. Now that I have children, it's clear that today Santa, as swell as he might be, inspires more greed than good behavior. Perhaps a little bit of Krampus might push some kiddies back onto the nice list!"

"Present arms!" Boss roars.

For the first time, the newcomers look scared. They finally notice all the old-timers' switches, all vicious and razor laced. They know they have been tricked.

Boss stomps towards the first of them and grabs the switch from his grasp.

"You had a full year to make this and all you got is a twig? This wouldn't cripple a cricket!" Boss drops the faulty switch and slaps his palm over the newbie's head. "Looks like you're on my list!"

Effortlessly, he yanks the newbie off the ground. The poor little bum only has time for his eyes to widen before getting crammed into Boss's slobbering mouth.

The other newbies realize what's happening and take off screaming; their crummy switches drop like bloody snowflakes.

Boss crunches a couple of bones before waving his hand. "Stop right there!"

The newbies freeze. You can tell by their tears that they're struggling to move but they haven't the strength to overcome the Boss's magic. On Christmas Eve, the Boss is the second most powerful being on Earth.

Boss could have made it quick for them, but that's not his way. Instead, he just struts down the line, picking out parts of the first newbie from his teeth, until he gets to me.

"Gimme that!" He grabs my switch out of my hand and holds it to his eye.

My switch is cut from the spine of a baby whale, dripping with spider venom, and cured in Klansman blood. It can rip through an elephant's hide, and it hurts just to look at it. I colored it red and white like a candy cane just to be in the spirit.

Boss still frowns. "I guess this isn't too lousy." He sticks it into his squirming sack and continues to Besserton.

Besserton spent his life abducting young women and taking them apart in his basement. Before his execution, he hand-crafted instruments of torture so vile that the policeman who discovered them went through years of vomiting and psychiatric therapy. But now Besserton is sweating as Boss inspects his switch.

"I seen better." Boss puts his face right against old Bessy. "You're just lucky we had so many first-timers this year."

Boss goes down the lines, inspecting switches and growling threats. He stops in front of Old Ozzie the Nazi and grins. "This switch won't do at all. I've always wondered how you'd taste."

He could have swallowed Ozzie in one bite but he stretches it out to eight. We knew one of us veterans was getting it this year, there had only been 99 new recruits last year.

After Ozzie, we relax a little. Sometimes Boss will surprise us and eat 101 souls or more, but this year, he just goes down the rest of the lines, stuffing switches in the sack. When he finishes, he starts eating the frozen newbies—he eases up his spell a little bit so they can beg. So that's our Christmas carols until the Adversary arrives on his sleigh and Boss leaves for another night of merriment.

"Poor Ozzie," Besserton sighs. Nobody else even pretends to care.

* * *

Boss gets back at daybreak and passes out. He's at his weakest now and there's always talk of rebellion. Nobody does nothing—all of us combined haven't got the muscle of a hamster. Even over a year, it's a strain just putting a single switch together. For all the fuss that Boss makes, demanding that we construct the switches for him, you'd think he'd give us enough energy to work.

The new recruits will be arriving soon. None of us say anything, but we're all hoping. Some years we get classes of 150 or more which means even newbies have a decent chance of surviving Christmas Eve.

A cloud starts to form at the mouth of the cave. Boss lurches up to greet it. Out of the mist, a group of new recruits comes stumbling—skinless, boneless misshapen souls, still praying and begging for mercy. "Help me, Jesus" and "Too young to die," indeed!

"Congratulations!" Boss calls out to them. "You worthy souls are invited to my workshop to make toys for good little children each Christmas!"

It's his little joke. He makes it every year and it never gets any funnier. But through the haze of the cloud, Boss appears enough like the Adversary to get a few of the newbie's hopes up.

He waits until the cloud completely dissipates and they get a good look at him. There's no hope anymore.

"Right! None of you are very worthy in the least. Each one of you committed the unpardonable sin of stealing Christmas presents and now you're mine. Forever! You owe me a switch and you got until next Christmas Eve to make it."

153

Boss yawns. "If you got any questions, ask one of them." He gestures to us as he walks back to his sack. As he passes, just before slumping down for his 12-month nap, he hisses to us: "Only 86!"

We stare at the recruits. Boss eats at least 100 of us every year. With only 86 recruits, 14 of us are doomed. Besserton is already in tears.

* * *

"Just do your best," all the old-timers tell the recruits. "You're already here. There's nothing old Krampus can do if your switch isn't perfect."

We do that every year—set up the newbies for failure, stacking the deck in our favor. But this year is different—more of us old-timers will be eaten than in memory. That isn't fair. Across the Christian world; there had to be more sinners stealing of Christmas presents than just these 86. Maybe people are better at protecting their gifts or perhaps some higher power saw fit to torment us even further.

Some souls get to thinking that getting eaten is an escape; some even ask to be eaten, believing it will be an end to their suffering. No such luck. If I went up to Boss right now and stuck my ear to his belly (and, believe it or not, Boss likes this), I'd hear old Ozzie and the rest of them screaming. Up to the end of the year, just before Boss goes to his outhouse, you can still hear them screaming inside of him. Then, and I know this from the times Boss sticks our heads in, they're still screaming in the hole . . . and that screaming goes on forever.

No, I don't want to be eaten.

Besserton sees me scribbling on a parchment and stops his work on his new switch.

"Why are you wasting time? You'd better start working."

I shrug. "I'm doing something more important than working."

Besserton gawks.

I get back to my writing. "I'm grass-root campaigning."

* * *

My mother was considered odd for giving Christmas presents, for celebrating Christmas in general. Years ago, Boston had outlawed Christmas celebrations, and, for most of the country, December 25 was still considered a work day.

Yet my mother gave gifts to even those who mocked her for it. But most of all she gave presents to my sister and me. Typically it was a single gift, unwrapped, very different from the experiences of spoiled children today. Unwrapped—that was why I saw the ring to begin with. That was why I came to Krampus.

The ring was simple garnet. My relatives often wore jewelry finer and more valuable, but the moment I saw it, I had to take it. I left my gift, an oak carving of an eagle in the cupboard, but crept to the garden and hid the ring beneath the rose bush.

I woke late for Christmas morning. My mother was rushing about the house, tearing open drawers, overturning furniture. She never suspected me, for what boy would fancy jewelry? Besides, I seemed out of sorts, as if I'd been beaten during the night with hellish switches not confined to my dreams.

In the spring, I dug for the ring but never found it. I had meant to sell it and start off into the world. In the end, it gained me nothing but switches for Krampus.

And yet, during my lifetime, switches became my calling. Long before the invention of the automobile, switches for steeds, slaves, hounds, and children were of high demand. Few men of my generation could sustain themselves simply crafting switches but I was regarded as a master. Fellow artisans looked upon my work with envy; boys in my neighborhood feared my name. The least of my switches was a bloody work of art. Even in my present state, if I slept, I could churn out greater switches than anyone else in the workshop. Over the years, I had made a backup switch for just such an occasion.

There would be no shortage of recruits when I was done.

My backup switch was flawless. Cut out of nightmare and midnight, laced with Satan's beard, a switch fit for Krampus's own backside—I'll have a year of peace while the others scramble.

While I lived, before the slave rebellion in Haiti, I traveled the trade routes and learned secrets that would have damned my soul even if I'd never touched my sister's ring. One of my wealthiest clients ruled over his plantation with knowledge that cursed men's souls. He tore open the veil between the living and the dead, called up spirits he called the loa, even commanding the dead to walk. While I never pursued these arts so intently, what I had learned could serve me well, even after death.

For years here in the workshop, I've been contacting the world of the living, whispering in the minds of politicians and businessmen. Before I only had time for the occasional persuasion, but now I had a year of full-time lobbying.

It wouldn't be hard. These men wanted to do what I whispered to them. They wanted to steal Christmas toys.

* * *

"You call this a switch?" Boss snarls. "Let me show you what it's worth."

The newbie never stops screaming as he slides down Boss's throat. Neither did Besserton when Boss rejected his switch. When he gets to me, I don't flinch.

"Let's . . ." His voice trails off. He stares, standing still longer than I've ever seen him, before mumbling something like "good job" and lurching to his next victim.

A bad Christmas Eve. The others don't know that their present is coming.

* * *

Boss had just settled down for his Christmas morn nap when the cloud arrives. The 85 other veterans look at it, pressing their fleshless lips together, nervously tapping their stumps. Then, Boss is standing up front, smirking and taking puffs from his pipe. He blows a smoke ring at the cloud just as it starts to open.

He drops the pipe when he sees what's inside.

Recruits pour out, hundreds upon hundreds, wailing and begging for mercy.

Boss forgets his usual joke; he has no idea what happened.

The Adversary is going to be surprised as well. His stinking deer will have the lightest load in memory.

Back when I was alive, Christmas was a work day. Laborers, even freemen, worked six days a week, 12 hours a day. A factory owner who gave his employees a half day for Christmas was considered a pansy.

It had been a challenge, but I planted those old ideas in the minds of millionaires and politicians. It saved them money so they bit. "Back to the Founding Fathers' dream," they'd proclaimed and pushed legislation to eliminate paid holidays and overtime pay.

This year, instead of exchanging gifts, mothers and fathers were at work. It was the greatest robbery of Christmas presents in history.

"We had to do it!" one of the recruits protests. "The company needed to be competitive!"

Boss lifts a finger to the side of his nose and grins. Next Christmas Eve, his sack will swell with switches. And Boss will be fatter and jollier than the Adversary ever was.

* * *

A Cincinnati resident, Mark Mills teaches composition and literature at Northern Kentucky University. He has published work in Necrotic Tissue, Tor.com, Brain Harvest, Short Story America, and Bards and Sages Quarterly. He has worked on and appeared in several local movies, including Evil Ambitions, Live Nude Shakespeare, Chickboxin' Underground, Zombie Cult Massacre, No Second Chances, and April's Fool. He currently is occupied with a large number of children, animals, and unpublished stories.

The Eleventh Night of Krampus:

THE GOD KILLER

by Cheresse Burke

Inspiration: When initially pondering this story, Cheresse was inclined to write some great Wu Xia-style martial arts sequence between a god and his assassin. Then she started thinking about how much people might want to kill the Gods, and how the Gods might deal with that in terms of a tribunal or court. The end result was slightly different from the initial conception.

Yes, I know why I'm here. I have my doubts that it'll make a difference, but I know.

And what do I care about you, all of you? What do I care about your grand tribunals, this whole circus? My testimony doesn't mean anything, you've already made that clear. Are you going to think about my choices; are you going to listen? Or is this testimony a formality before I receive my sentence?

Well, I think my path was clear, from the moment I stepped down that passage. You can call me the God killer if you want, but you can at least reserve judgment of my person until I'm finished here. Then you can decide what sort of eternal torment I should get at the hands of . . . well, whatever. Whatever you are. No, I won't call you gods. *Real* gods are responsible. *Real* gods care. But you decide the fate of the world without asking whether the world has a say.

Krampus isn't—wasn't—a real god either, was he? Demigod, I guess you'd call him. People hardly even believe in him anymore. It's easier to believe in Santa, I guess. It's that positive reinforcement thing. Everybody wants to be good for Santa, and nobody cares about not being bad for Krampus. But he had some power, right up to the end.

I used to watch those two in the cold winter months. That's how I found out that I was different, that I was a Watcher. That I could see demigods as they went about their business on Earth. When I was a kid I would run up to the attic whenever Mama had a fight with one of her boyfriends. I would crouch at the windowsill and make up stories for all the bums drifting by. They had routines as regular as the canal boats. The jolly fat man and his friend were no different, meandering past my window at the same time every night. They would walk with their heads tilted toward each other, deep in conversation. They passed jokes back and forth, and sometimes they passed a bottle as well. The tall man and the short man. The young man and the old one. A devil and a saint.

You wouldn't expect them to be chums, would you? The man who spoils kids and the one that brings them down to Hell. But they laughed together. Old Nick had a booming voice that crashed over the water and exploded on the roofs around our apartment building, splashing the air around us with his mirth. I thought the whole world must be able to hear him laugh. Krampus, though, his laugh was quieter, darker, a low chuckle that made its way into the cracks and the corners of the world. It was the laugh that made you stop, look around, convince yourself that you were alone and safe.

I read about Krampus, when I was around nine or 10. Just after I'd realized who I was watching tramp around on the canals. The stories say that he carried around a wicker sack. What bullshit. He was always dressed impeccably, like the richest banker in Amsterdam. He wouldn't have been caught *dead* carrying a wicker basket around. He didn't need it, anyway.

I hated them both. They scared me when I was a child, and shouldn't they have? It was obvious that no one else saw them. I often saw beggars and drunks pass them in the street with less notice than they'd give to a piece of rubbish. No one else ever mentioned the two men, not even my friends who sometimes sat with me in the attic when they were visiting and Mama's boyfriend of the week came by. I figured it out pretty quickly. I didn't talk about them, I pretended that I didn't see them. I *wished* I didn't see them.

I got my wish when I moved out of Mama's apartment. They disappeared from view, and didn't reappear for a long, long time. Maybe that's why I was so curious when I caught sight of the tall one again. I had wondered for years whether I had hallucinated everything, whether I was one step away from singing to the canals and cringing in the straightjacket. I was *relieved* when I saw him. I guess that's why things happened the way they did.

That night I saw him, the night you're all so keen to know about, I only saw him because I'd gone out of my way. I'd had a fight—another fight. I was fired, this time. You people do know what that means, don't you? I mean, can gods even get fired? Anyway, I was. I worked under a sous chef and I was sick of his petty rules and thunderous temper. When it came to his word against mine, I was out on my ass, no big shock there. So I packed up my knives and I took the long route home through the snowfall. I've always liked walking in the snow.

I stormed along, shivering more with anger than with cold. Swearing to myself from time to time, going over the whole spectacle again and again in my head. I let my feet do all the thinking for me, and bowed my head, and just kept going. By the time I noticed him, we were nearly touching noses. I started and stared into eyes as blue as the heart of a flame. Then I hopped out of the way and even said, "Excuse me," in the nicest tone I could manage. He just kept going. No noise, no pause, nothing. I turned after him, maybe with half a mind to shout something. All those thoughts were torn away like snowflakes in the wind as I turned to stare after his retreating back.

The tall thin man with midnight skin, with black horns, with cloven hooves. The walking myth and icon from my childhood.

Like I said before, I was giddy with relief. I'm not just being fancy here, so you can stop rolling your eyes—you, over there in the toga. Maybe you don't know what it's like, to think you might need institutionalization. To think you're so crazy you can't trust what you see, what you feel, what you hear. Of course you don't think that. In your perfect little world, you're always right. But *I* was glad, in a way. Glad that I was sane, that he was real, even though I remembered his laugh and how it could chill me.

I should have been smart enough to stay away from him, I know that. But I was overwhelmed by all of those different emotions: relief and elation, anger and self-righteousness, and even curiosity. I used to watch that man go round and round with his fat friend, trading jokes and drinking booze so strong it could fuel a barge. This time, I noticed that Nick wasn't beside him, or even close behind, nor did Krampus walk with that relaxed, meandering gait that he used when taking a stroll with his friend. He walked with purpose now. With a mission. I suddenly cared about what he did when he was working, about where he went and who he *really* was. And I know I shouldn't have, but I started to follow him.

At first I was quiet about it, I didn't want to get caught. I couldn't help thinking about those goat horns, about how they'd feel, cold and snow-kissed, sliding through my windpipe. But, well, maybe he was deaf. Or maybe that same power that lets me see his kind also kept him from seeing me. When I figured out that he didn't notice me, I got a lot bolder. I just walked behind him, with my eyes fixed firmly on his back. It was perfect. Nobody else saw him and passers-by assumed that I had a purpose, a goal of some kind. In reality I couldn't think past that figure in front of me. All that angry energy that had led me to this meeting, it had turned into some ridiculous, childish excitement. I could hardly keep from skipping, hopping or tilting my head back and whooping out to the world. I could have done it, I guess. He wouldn't have seen me, and to everyone else I would have been just another weirdo.

I followed him down side streets that twisted and curved. He wasn't at all the jovial creature that I'd seen passing the bottle to Old Nick. He didn't laugh, didn't booze, and though he seemed to move with no sense of destination, there was definitely something of a purpose to his steps. I followed him for around 15 minutes before his pattern took on any sort of meaning.

We'd come far from the canals and wandered to a dirty street lined with graffitied brown brick apartments. Krampus stepped delicately around cans and old burger wrappings that created little hills under the snow. I tramped through them.

He stopped at the gate of a small apartment complex, then opened it and slipped through, so quickly that I didn't have time to follow. Even though I hadn't seen a key in his hand, the gate was firmly locked and did nothing more than rattle when I pushed at it. Krampus paused at the noise, and glanced back, and for a moment my blood turned to snow. I was certain he'd seen me, or heard me. But he only turned, and walked away from the gate and into one of the apartment buildings.

I was worried that he lived there, that I had followed him all this way for nothing. I hung around for a while, hoping that he'd come out, that someone else might go in, that no one would call the police on my loitering, that I hadn't just hallucinated another episode with the Devil-Man.

When you're waiting for something, time always seems too slow, so that you can have about a million paranoid thoughts per minute. So even though I was convinced it had been an hour, I can't have been waiting long. I hadn't yet pulled myself away when he came back and opened up the gate.

He herded five dazed children in front of him, out of the apartment complex and onto the street. I'd say they were in the five to seven age range, if I had to guess. But I haven't had kids, and I was an only child. So don't sue me if I'm wrong.

As soon as I saw those kids, all the hairs on the back of my arms stood up. On end. They just looked . . . wrong. Like they were all sick or doped or something. They swayed like they were off-balance, and their eyes were glazed. Weirdest of all, they just *stood* there. Maybe that doesn't impress you too much, but anyone who ever observed anything about kids knows that they act like baby elephants with ADHD. They don't stand around like they're in a trance, and they don't keep quiet, especially when there's nothing interesting to be looking at. And believe me, there's nothing of note anywhere in that neighborhood. No, they were all entranced by the shadowy figure that stepped out from the apartment gate. When he started to walk down the street, they all followed, like little ducks in a row after their great horned mama duck.

If any of you cared about humans, about kids, you wouldn't be wondering why I followed him after that. I *knew* something was gonna happen with those kids. So there we went, down each street. He must have done something to make the kids invisible, too, because no one wanted to know what a little troop of screamers was doing wandering around in the middle of the night. He never looked left or right, or even behind to make sure that they were all with him. He just walked, and walked. Every so often he'd stop, disappear inside a building, and pick up some more. I could never get in after him, not until the last. He was always too quick, slipping around the side of the gate and letting it lock after him. But finally I got my chance.

He had 14 kids when he moved in on the last. Yes, 14 exactly. I counted, I knew it was important. That fifteenth kid, he lived on the bottom of one of the old apartment buildings, most in need of renovation. Those old ones didn't have gates, anyone could wander in. The window was open, and I could hear him screaming at his mother. It was a raw, angry sound, without words, and he wouldn't stop no matter what she tried.

Well, the big guy stopped, and cocked his head, and listened. Behind him 14 children swayed in the snow. They didn't cry or complain, they didn't even shiver. And then there was me.

I don't think that he intended to get any more kids that night, but when he heard that one, he made a quick decision. He swung the front door wide open and went inside. This time, I was ready for him. I caught the edge of the door and swung round it. It didn't even double back, not that he'd checked. But I was in.

He walked right up to the apartment door and rapped, three times. The sound was crisp and clean and loud, and even normal people must have heard it, because soon after I could hear footsteps approaching the door. Krampus put his hand in his pocket, then drew it back out as a closed fist. When the door jerked open and the mother's mousy, dirty face peered out from behind the rape chain, Krampus brought his fist up to the level of her eyes, uncurled his strong fingers, and blew something from his hand into her face with a powerful huff.

She tried to twist away, but she wasn't quick enough. A strange, shining powder settled over her cheeks and the bridge of her nose, on her eyelashes and around her thin lips. Some must have gotten into her eyes or nose, maybe her mouth. I couldn't see that much in the thin strip between the frame and the door. But he managed to get her somehow, because her face went slack and her eyes dulled, and she turned away from the door without closing it. Without saying anything, or hearing anything.

I could tell when she picked up the kid. His voice rose and he started wailing and beating at her. His fists thumped against her clothes, her bare skin. She just ignored him, though, and she came right up to the door and undid the rape chain and Krampus blew his strange powder in the kid's face, and suddenly the kid got all docile, like a marionette without strings. He slid from his mother's limp hands and stood at the door, waiting for his new master. He followed Krampus just like all the others, out the door and down the street in a neat little line with me at the end.

I'm not sure why I didn't stop things right there. I guess I could have. But I'm no cold-blooded killer. I was horrified. Maybe a little fascinated. But I wasn't angry, yet.

We traipsed along for another 20 minutes, until we came to an abandoned building. Maybe it used to hold one bankrupt firm or another, or maybe it had always looked that way—uninteresting, worthless. Safe for Krampus. All the glass in the bottom row of windows was gone, the rooms inside were dark and empty. I doubt the door security worked, but Krampus didn't even try. He went around the corner to a side door and opened it without a key. He had to hold it open until all the kids could get through, and I managed to squeeze in beside the seventh.

We found ourselves in a gray service stairwell, lit only by the dirty fluorescent lamps that illumine all such stairwells. He started to descend, and we followed. Down and down we went, floor after floor, silently trooping. When we started, my fleet slapped and echoed so loudly in the concrete space that my fear of discovery was renewed. But Krampus still didn't notice. To him, I simply didn't exist.

I can't say how far down we went. It was a long way, it felt like forever. By the time we got to the bottom, my feet didn't echo on the stairs anymore. I didn't make any sound, actually. I couldn't even hear myself breathe. We finally came to a door, the only one I'd seen on the stairwell since we'd entered the building. Krampus opened it, and held it open as his little captives shambled through. I squeezed in with the seventh child again. I think I jostled him a little bit. He stumbled and my whole body flushed with wild paranoia. And he looked at me, I swear he looked right at me—and through me, to whatever was behind.

I guess this is where we get into the big problems between me and you, isn't it? I suppose you would have just left them there.

Someone told me once that people didn't think of Hell as a hot place until Dante's *Inferno* became a classic. But Dante only wrote of Purgatory as a fiery pit. Where everyone got their sins burned away.

This was not purgatory. It was as cold as ice, down in Krampus' lair. Everything was grey, as if carved from stone—what kind of stone sits under Amsterdam? And I could see, even though there was no light. It was like the walls themselves pushed out their grayness until that was all you could look at. That, and the kids. And the cages.

I don't care how bad they'd been. Who does that to kids? Their cages lined a long, straight path, made from the same gray material as the rest of this world, round like eggs, or cocoons. The cages had been fashioned into bars, so that they could see out. So that they could see what stalked toward them, past cage after cage where the shivering brats huddled together, three or four cramped in where even one would have had to stoop. I guess his powder wore off eventually, because these weren't little zombies anymore. They cried, some loudly, some softly. A few screamed, until they saw him coming. Then their voices seemed to fail them, and they began to shake. Some of them pissed themselves. And I could see them close their eyes as he went past, twist their lips into silent prayers. What were they thinking? Who were they praying to?

Some of them saw me. Their eyes grew wide, and their mouths stopped moving long enough to form a perfect O. But they didn't cry out. Maybe they knew instinctively that I wasn't like him. Just to make sure, I put my finger up to my lips.

I had been afraid before. A little afraid, and shamefully curious. Not so, now. Now I was enraged, enraged enough to kill someone.

I took out my case of knives and picked the biggest one. I'd never stabbed someone, not before him, but I'd done plenty of chopping, hacking, sawing, slicing . . . you do that, when you're a cook.

I aimed for the spinal cord. Figured that since he looked . . . well, almost like the rest of us did, he might have the same weak spots.

I don't have to tell you exactly how I did it. I don't really want to think about it. Do you think I'm proud of murdering a demi-god? With those young faces, staring? I'm not like one of your old heroes, I don't expect songs around the fire. I'm a cook, not a butcher. And giving these kids trauma to carry around for the rest of their lives? Well, they probably already had those. But I don't doubt I made them worse.

The first time I chopped I got it wrong, I knew it as soon as I swung. It cut through his immaculate suit and hacked into his spine at an angle. He let out a roar like a bull, threw his head back. His sharp horns gleamed in the strange, gloomy light of his lair. If you'd seen those horns like I had, if you'd realized what they might do to you if you weren't quick enough, you wouldn't wonder why that cave was a study in scarlet, a butcher's floor. People do terrible things when they're terrified. And we don't like it afterwards, we don't brag. We try to be calm, cool, for the sake of the kids.

No surprise that they didn't want to come with me. I found keys in his pocket, after I found his pocket, and eventually the key to the cages. The same old skeleton key for every cage. Not very good security, but a distinctive kind of personality, elegance, antiquity. Like its late owner, I suppose.

They couldn't bear to look at me, let alone follow me, and I couldn't blame them. I must have looked like another kind of demon. I left the door propped open when I left, and I climbed up the forever stairway, back to reality. Back to the world. I told myself it was probably best that they didn't come out behind me. Imagine explaining to a bunch of policemen why I was covered in blood with 30 or so missing kids.

Of course, I didn't think I'd end up here, either.

So there you are. Can you judge me? Do you have the capacity? Have any of you known fear, compassion, or horror? Do you understand the need to protect lives other than your own? Can gods really empathize with us mere mortals? Or has your power over life, death rendered you so far above it all that you don't understand me, even now?

Well, cast your judgment, then. I don't fear it.

* * *

Cheresse Burke lives and works in Copenhagen, Denmark. In her spare time she reads submissions for *Grimdark Magazine,* and writes short stories and novels. "The God Killer" is her first published short story.

The Twelfth Night of Krampus:

A KRAMPUS CAROL
by Scott Farrell

Inspiration: Scott loves all sorts of off-beat, quirky ethnic and regional holiday traditions, from Caga Tio to the Viking Sunwheel and, of course, the Krampus. For years, he has diligently maintained a Facebook page called "Americans Who Love Krampus," despite the fact that many of his friends and family members think celebrating the holidays with songs, decorations, and depictions of a horned demon is a little crazy. Scott will proudly be wearing his "Happy Krampus Day" tee shirt this Christmas morning, just like he does each year.

Santa's sleigh seemed to have come down in a crash landing, leaving packages scattered all over the lawn. Eight plastic reindeer, freed from their harnesses, were humping one another. Santa himself was face down in a snow bank with his robe hitched up 'round his jolly ol' bowl full of jelly, and a staff of holly shoved up his keester.

Not even a week into December, and that little bastard who lived on the corner had literally turned Christmas into a wreck.

John Nast ran a hand over his buzz-cut white hair as he shook his head in disgust, surveying the debris of what, just the night before, had been his holiday lawn ornaments. The very same ornaments his late wife, Maggie, had loved so much.

The latest masterpiece in petty vandalism from Chad Brooks, John thought. Somebody's gotta take charge and bring this to a stop. Drastic measures were needed, and John had a few in mind.

This had been going on for a year now, since last December, when the Brooks family moved into the house on the corner of River Street, three doors down from John's place. The real estate agent had welcomed them to the neighborhood with a big red Christmas bow on the door, like the beginning of one of those "very special" movies Maggie always got him to sit through on the Hallmark Channel. When Maggie had been diagnosed with breast cancer three years ago, he'd lost count of the number of those shows he'd watched to make her happy. Probably hundreds, stuck in one of those damned uncomfortable hospital chairs at her bedside, half hoping she'd fall asleep so he could quietly switch the TV to a Pirates game or a good ol' war movie. He knew those corny stories about big-city families moving out to farm country and charming the locals were a load of crap, and the arrival of the Brooks trio into this quiet Butler Township neighborhood was proof of that.

They'd pulled up in their minivan, right off the pike from Philadelphia, a rolling demonstration of John's long-held claim that city parents had no idea how to raise kids. Let them do nothing but watch the boob tube and play their video games, and call it discipline when you give them a "time out." John would've bet that was exactly how things went in the Brooks household.

From the moment they pulled in the driveway he'd spotted the clues. The bread-winner of the family, Arnold, had been making a call on his cell phone even before he'd gotten his seat belt unbuckled. The realtor had mentioned that Mr. Brooks was relocating because he had hired on with a legal firm in Pittsburgh. He was a defense attorney, which meant John had cause to dislike Arnold even before he laid eyes on him. Seeing him in his prissy clothes and his beauty-parlor perfect hair only sealed the deal.

As the van's doors opened, Arnold's wife, Katie, had made some kind of sarcastic remark. John was too far away to hear her words, but he could detect the woman's disapproving attitude in her body language. She went to the back of the van and started unloading the stack of heavy boxes, a job Arnold didn't even look like he was thinking about helping her with. As he walked up the front steps of his new house, Arnold barely took the time to glare down the block and acknowledge John with a little snort and a shake of his head. Guess that was how folks from Philly said, "Howdy, neighbor!"

That left Chad sulking alone in the back seat of the van with a set of those ridiculous, tiny headphones jammed in his ears like two spaghetti noodles. He must've sat there for half an hour—John kept tabs on things from his front porch—not even so much as making eye contact with either of his parents. Like getting a nice, new house for Christmas was the biggest inconvenience imaginable.

When the boy finally dragged himself out of the backseat, John watched him go moping inside, his long, brown hair drooping into his eyes and tails of his flannel shirt untucked, hardly even bothering to pick his feet up off the ground. Didn't even take a moment to glance down the street and give a nod "hello." At least his old man had had the courtesy to acknowledge John with a dirty look.

Yes, the Brooks' arrival on River Street had been unpleasantly memorable. But hardly a week after that, things had gotten ugly real fast. The first shot in this year-long battle had been fired.

It started with that snowman, the one John's grandson, Mark, had made when Nina and her husband Frank had come for Christmas dinner. They lived in an apartment in downtown Pittsburgh, near the bank where Frank worked, and little Mark was always delighted to come to his "Paw-Paw's" house where he had a real yard to play in. Little guy'd spent a whole afternoon building that snowman. It put a smile on John's face when he woke up—promptly at 5:35, each and every morning—took his cup of coffee out on the porch, and saw it standing there looking out over River Street.

But in the cold, pre-dawn light on New Year's Day John saw the snowman had gotten some sort of makeover. Frosty's hat and stick nose had been tossed away, and his whole head was bright red. His now-armless body was colored dark brown, and there was a thick pattern of black curls around its base.

As the sun broke over the horizon, John recognized what he was looking at: someone had used spray paint to turn Mark's snowman into a giant snow boner in the middle of the night.

John didn't holler, he didn't swear, he didn't go on a rampage. He just folded his thick, muscled arms, gave the thing a good long looking at, and let his investigative instincts take over. None of the kids around here have ever done something like this before, he thought. So what's changed? What's different? What new element's been added to the equation?

Then he looked down the street, and he had his answer: Chad Brooks. Troublemaker.

John tried to get rid of it, but he had to hand it to the kid: This was one well-executed prank. As a result of a sunny afternoon and a few nights of freezing temperatures, the surface of the snowman was iced over good. The thing was too solid to dismantle with a shovel, and trying to hose the paint off just turned it all into a horrific, multicolored mess. By the time the neighbors were awake, John had realized that his yard was going to look like Picasso had thrown up there for weeks.

All courtesy of the new kid on the block.

Now, a year later, surveying the obscene remains of his Christmas yard display, John saw a road running straight from the snowman spray-painting incident, through a year's worth of firecrackers in his mailbox, toilet paper in his trees, and smashed pumpkins on his doorstep, to this. And he realized it was time to do something, to make that kid finally realize that when you mess with the big dog, you're gonna get bit in the end.

Time to introduce Chad Brooks to the Krampus.

* * *

John rooted around in the back of his closet for his heavy parka, the old military surplus one he'd gotten for their vacation to Colorado, with coyote fur around the hood and cuffs. Maggie always hated that coat, said it made him look like a mangy stray dog.

It would be just perfect for the Krampus.

John had first heard about the Krampus at his grandfather's knee. Grandpa Nast had come from the old country, and had a German accent as thick as dark rye bread. Around the holidays, when other kids were learning stories of Rudolph and the Little Drummer Boy, Grandpa Nast told John and his younger brother, Eric, about Krampus: the furry, horned devil-man who came to swat little kids with a switch. He'd make them scream and cry, then he'd chain them up, put them in his sack, and drag them down to the lake to drown.

"Und hif you are diso-pee-diant, talking back to your mama and dees-respecting your elders, das Krampus will come to visit you und . . ." then Grandpa Nast slammed his hand down on the arm of his chair with a bang. "There vill be beating! He vill rip your skin and bite your flesh vith his teeth, and throw you in freezing water. Then that is where you vill spend your Christmas."

After that, John and Eric exhibited nothing but their best behavior whenever Grandpa Nast came to visit.

But other times, when Grandpa Nast wasn't around, John's attitude about the Krampus changed a little. He didn't sound quite so terrifying. In fact, he seemed pretty cool, putting kids in chains. No one messed with Krampus, just like no one messed with Grandpa Nast. They got respect.

And young John wanted people to respect him, too.

So, one December night he'd gone to the closet and gotten an old, fuzzy gray sweater and wrapped it around his head and shoulders. Then he'd found an old dog collar in the garage, and rolled the morning newspaper into a stout tube. And then, on tiptoe, he'd gone quietly into his brother's bedroom and woken him with a whap of the rolled-up newspaper on his dresser.

When Eric opened his eyes he saw the hairy silhouette at his bedside and heard the jingling dog chain, and he screamed bloody murder. By the time his parents came out of their room to find out what was the matter, John was already back in his own bed with his Krampus props stashed under his covers.

Through the wall, John heard his mother's voice. "Eric's had a pretty bad dream."

"I don't doubt it," his father answered. "Pop's been telling the boys those horrible old German stories. Christmas isn't a time for monsters."

Eric was still young. If it ever entered his head that it was really John, and not the Krampus, in his room, he never mentioned it. For years, any time John wanted to coerce his little brother into something, all he needed to say was, "Krampus will come to take you away if you don't listen to me," and Eric was instantly cooperative. In John's book, that was respect.

Now, it was time for young Chad Brooks to get a taste of that. Only Chad wasn't an innocent little boy snoozing with visions of sugarplums in his head. He was a jaded, teenaged delinquent, and he was about to learn that even in a quiet neighborhood like River Street, there were things that could scare some respect into a young man.

* * *

John's old "cop junk," as Maggie used to call it, was stored beneath the tool bench in his garage. He'd packed it all away when he retired from the force. Ten years on, everything was faded, tarnished, and wrinkled. But what he was looking for wasn't in the boxes of old uniforms, duty logs, and other clutter waiting to be thrown out. What he wanted was that one chest full of the things that had been his day-to-day carrying gear when he was on the job.

John had spent his whole career on the highway patrol unit of the Pennsylvania State Police Force. No cushy desk job; he found field work particularly rewarding. It warmed his heart whenever he got to help a family whose car had overheated on their summer road trip, or come to the rescue of a senior citizen who'd hit a patch of ice on a freezing night. Lots of, "Thank you, officer!" and "I don't know what we'd've done without you." Good for the karma.

But he also liked going hands-on with belligerent drunks who'd been pulled over for swerving on the highway, and getting into chases with vehicles driven by suspects in robberies or assaults.

John was a big man, with the build of an Austrian railroad worker. In his time on the force, none of the suspects he'd taken into custody had ever gotten the better of him. Oh, there were a few times when he'd gone to the pavement, and he had absorbed his fair share of punches. But he had always given as good as he got. If he got hauled to the emergency ward, he made sure the fellow who'd put the hurt on him was in the next gurney.

Of course, that wasn't what he was going to do to Chad Brooks. He wanted to scare the boy straight, not damage him. Not permanently, at least. Just give him something to think about, and John had a method for doing that.

One of the perennial problems for highway patrol officers, especially around prom and homecoming times, were cars crammed full of kids who'd somehow gotten hold of a few six packs, and went out to have their first taste of playing grown up: racing along, hanging out the windows, swerving all over the road, and generally making dangerous nuisances of themselves.

You made a stop like that, there were a few ways things could play out. You might just let the kids off with a warning if they seemed contrite or embarrassed enough when you demanded their license and registration. If they tried to play it cool, you could haul them down to the county drunk tank on a reckless endangerment charge. A few hours behind bars, resting on a mattress that smelled of puke and urine, was an experience guaranteed to melt even the coolest of punk attitudes.

But now and again you came across a particular kind of kid, who didn't seem to be at all disturbed by a run-in with the law. And that probably meant they'd grown up with parents who didn't give a solitary crap what sort of trouble they got themselves into. Kids like were damned near immune to any sort of official punishment the police could dish out.

In those cases, John and his fellow officers had something off-the-radar. Something John liked to think of as, "the Krampus treatment."

It went like this: You put the kids in the back of your patrol car, ignored their pleas and demands to know what was going on, drove them to one of the deserted stretches of feeder road that every PSP highway patrolman knew about, well out of view of the Interstate. That was when things got interesting.

You started by stripping them to their skivvies, cuffing their hands behind their backs, and blinding them with one of the heavy-duty squad car spotlights. Then a couple of officers dressed in their riot gear, with faces hidden by their balaclavas, came at the kids with their billy clubs out looking like nothing in the world would get them off faster than cracking a few skulls.

And for the otherwise unreachable hard-cases, John and his fellow officers had one last ace in the hole: a few pepper spray canisters that had reached their expiration date, and had been salvaged from the disposal bin while the supply officer was conveniently on a coffee break. Give those kids a little snort of that shit and let them spend the next half hour sneezing and hacking while those big, black-masked officers pounded the bumpers of the patrol cars with their batons just an inch or two from the kids' heads, and screamed obscenities right in their puffy, snot-covered faces. No teenager in existence was so tough that *that* didn't put the fear of God and Uncle Sam into them.

And the final act in this drama came just at that moment when the kids were convinced that they were going to get beaten to death and dumped in an unmarked grave somewhere. Then John would unsnap his holster and watch their eyes go wide. But instead of drawing his revolver, John pulled out a little piece of paper that showed a dancing, horned devil, wagging his long, curly tongue, and leading a couple of crying kids on a chain. It was a *Krampuskarten*—something his grandfather had told him about, a little seasonal memento for people who needed a reminder about the value of respect and good behavior.

Each card had Krampus and his victims drawn in a different pose, but they were all emblazoned with the same three words: *Gruss vom Krampus!* (Which translated, as Grandpa Nast explained, "Cheers, from das Krampus!")

"You got off easy this time," John would say in an almost congratulatory way as the other officers unlocked the cuffs and tossed the kids' clothes down on the pavement. "If we catch you again, this is going to go a whole lot worse for you. You hear?"

As they were sucking up their last few sobs and hurriedly yanking their pants back on, the kids would inevitably thank the officers for their kindness and promise they'd be absolute frickin' angels for the rest of their lives.

By the time John and his fellow officers got the kids back to their vehicles, the pepper spray was all worn off, and only the humiliation and terror remained. But their Gruss vom Krampus cards were small, and completely untraceable souvenirs. If there were any claims about police misconduct, it would come down to the sworn oaths of half a dozen decorated patrol officers against the crazy-sounding allegations of teenagers who shouldn't have been out drinking and joyriding anyway.

"The Krampus treatment" was how you took care of the worst kind of disrespectful kids.

Things like GPS trackers and dash-mounted video cameras had put an end to going "off the radar" for John and his brother officers. But now, in retirement, the memories of those terrified, pleading teenagers gave John some ideas about how to deal with Chad Brooks. He'd already tried confronting the boy directly about all of his destructive neighborhood shenanigans. But Chad was mighty good at leaving no scrap of evidence behind that John could use to legitimately pin the boy down with.

The few times John had gotten fed up enough to go tell Arnold to get his kid under control, the kid's father proved to be as irresponsible as his son. "You leave Chad out of this, Nast," he demanded. "He isn't causing any of your problems and you can't prove otherwise. Maybe you ought to think about who you pissed off, instead of trying to blame my boy." Weaseling out of things with technicalities and counter-accusations. What else would you expect from a defense attorney?

Okay then, it was up to John himself to fix this problem, to give Chad Brooks a little lesson in respect that his parents were clearly incapable of teaching him.

In the cold evening air of his garage, John went through box after box, stacking them up on his workbench until he got to his old footlocker. The hinge creaked dryly as he opened it, and he saw that this was the box he was looking for.

Right on top was that old photo he used to keep stuck to the dash of his patrol car—Christ, Maggie practically looked like a teenager! She'd written on it, "Come home safe to me!" and had signed her name with a great big heart beside her face. John admired the faded photo for a minute, then gently put it aside as he lifted his old duty belt out of the chest.

He had to tug at the pouch snap several times before he got it unfastened. Finally it popped and he slid out a little device that looked like a cross between a flashlight and a Martian ray gun.

The LED indicator on top was yellow, a "low battery" warning. Not surprising, John thought, after sitting in storage for so many years.

But when he punched the "test" button, the Taser's forward prongs crackled with an electrical arc. Enough juice there to get the job done.

Grandpa Nast had said that the Krampus carried a birch switch, a narrow, thorny rod that would leave bright red welts across your ass when he hit you with it. This wouldn't leave any welts, but John knew that when he pulled that trigger, Chad was going to stand up like he was watching a Fourth of friggin' July parade go past. You didn't slouch and drag your feet when you were getting motivated by 50,000 volts.

After that, he'd bet that Chad wouldn't think it was much fun to screw with people's holiday celebrations on River Street ever again.

* * *

John hadn't bothered to straighten up the mess in his front yard. He wanted the neighbors to get a good look at that scene in the daylight, so there'd be no bellyaching if someone caught wind of what was about to happen to Chad. Now, as John left his garage just after sundown, the sight of it filled him, you might say, with the Krampus spirit.

He stood at the top of the driveway, concealed by the shadow of the eaves. Better to stay out of sight as things went down, even though he suspected he was only going to accomplish what everyone else on River Street wished they had the gumption to do.

As he looked over the wreckage of his Christmas décor, he noticed something he hadn't caught before. On the edge of that upside-down sleigh there'd been two oversized Christmas stockings, one with his name written in gold on the top, and another that said "Maggie." When she was alive, they'd hung those stockings on their mantle each Christmas. But when she passed away, he decided to put them on the edge of the sleigh, so everyone who walked by his house during the season would remember her name.

Now, after Chad's little rampage, John saw only one of those stockings lying limply on the snow-covered yard; the one that read

"John" on the cuff. Maggie's was missing, and the thought of that infuriated John even more. He couldn't abide the notion of Chad Brooks' dirty little hand clutching his late wife's Christmas stocking. If John had any reservations about giving Chad the Krampus treatment, they vanished in that instant. What he was about to do was mild compared to what that little punk deserved.

Stepping into the glow of the porch light for just a moment, John reached out and yanked the branch of holly out of Santa's rear end. Then he retreated to the shadows by the driveway once more.

He slid the black police balaclava over his face, pulled up the furry hood of his army parka, and gave the length of holly a test swing. The sharp, thorny leaves cut the air with an intimidating, satisfying hiss.

And in his other hand, tucked into his coat pocket, rested the little Taser unit.

John hadn't given much thought to how, exactly, he was going to get to Chad. He couldn't exactly walk up and ring the doorbell. He simply had a notion that if he was patient and stealthy, an opportunity would present itself.

And now, just as he stood at the edge of the driveway in the shadow of his porch light, he heard soft footsteps coming down the sidewalk, footsteps made by someone who barely bothered to pick up his own feet. It was like a gift to him dropped out of Santa's big red sack.

Here came Chad Brooks, right back to the scene of the Christmas crime.

John backed away and stood stock-still in the darkness by his garage. He kept an eagle eye on Chad as the boy approached down the sidewalk, stopped in front of the house and turned to look at the mess on the lawn. Admiring his work one last time, no doubt.

John was invisible there in the dark, and he knew he had to get Chad out of sight of the neighbors before he started things. As Chad stared at John's yard, probably having himself a good chuckle, John let out a soft, "Hssst," to get his attention.

Chad turned toward the sound and squinted. "Mr. Nast? Is that you?" he called. Dumb-ass kid was standing right in the glare of the streetlight. John knew he could practically do jumping jacks and the kid wouldn't be able to see him in the shadows.

But as luck would have it, Chad's curiosity got the better of him. Or maybe he just thought he'd get an extra kick out of laughing in the face of the doddering old man whose decorations he'd ruined. In either case, John grinned just a little under his black facemask as Chad started walking cautiously up the driveway, right toward the place where he was hiding.

The side gate creaked ever-so-slightly as John eased himself into the back yard. If that kid followed him here, they'd be completely hidden from the street. And, sure enough, Chad had the hook in his mouth and John was reeling him right in.

"Mr. Nast? You back here?" the boy wondered quietly as he pushed the gate open. "Mr. Nast, I gotta to talk to you."

Chad came round the corner of the garage and found himself looking at a large, hairy, faceless figure with a long, leafy switch in its upraised hand. He hardly had time to register what he was seeing, to gasp and wonder, "What?" before the branch came down and left a stinging welt across the side of his neck.

Drawn up to his full height, John was a full foot taller than Chad. The sight of the boy's wide, panic-filled eyes warmed John like a sip from a cup of eggnog. He was glad that the balaclava concealed his face. It wouldn't be nearly as terrifying to be attacked by a Krampus with a big crap-eatin' grin on his face.

Chad tried to sputter out a few words. John cut him off with an enraged, wordless howl as he raised his holly switch for another blow. The boy scrambled backwards, tripped over his own shoes (that would teach the damned kid to pick up his feet!) and hit the ground ass first. As the boy made a clumsy dash for the gate on all fours, John delivered another lash with the branch right across the back of both knees.

The blow put Chad right back down into the slushy gravel on the dark walkway.

As Chad scuttled along the ground like the rat that he was, John could see that the boy would be out the gate and back into the street in just a few seconds. Kid was so scared that he'd probably pissed himself already. This was just the moment John had been waiting for.

He plunged his hand into the pocket of his parka and pulled out the Taser.

It was nearly impossible to aim the thing in the dark, but the Taser wasn't a sharpshooter's weapon. John just extended his arm and pulled the trigger, sending the trio of barbs darting forward on the end of their hair-fine lead wires.

An instant later he heard the rattlesnake crack of the electrical charge as the tips came alive. Eerie halos of micro-lightning danced between the contact points, lighting up the darkened yard in a pulsing, bright blue flash.

Chad whirled like a marionette in a windstorm. He fumbled with the latch for a moment, shouted, "Sh-sh-shit!" then tore open the gate and sprinted away.

The Taser leads dropped to the ground as John released the weapon's trigger. Had he hit Chad with the contact barbs? He didn't know, and he wasn't sure it really mattered.

What he did know was that that kid had come to smirk, gloat, and admire the job of Christmas vandalism he'd done.

And he'd left in a terrified, painful, piss-soaked panic.

Another triumph for the Krampus treatment! Worked like a charm every time.

Listening to the sound of Chad's footsteps dashing through the snow, slipping and falling on every sidewalk crack and patch of ice, John leaned the holly branch against his garage wall and had himself a good, long Christmas laugh.

Ho, ho, friggin' ho!

* * *

John knelt in front of his workbench and laid the black balaclava back in the trunk. Before replacing the Taser in its holster, he popped off the electrode unit on the front and carefully coiled the tiny wires around his hand. Early tomorrow morning, he thought, he'd have to go over to the Target at the mall in Butler and get rid of that in the store's dumpster. His deniability would be shot to hell if someone spotted Taser wires dangling out of his trash can on pick-up day.

John was carefully stuffing the spent Taser cartridge out of sight when he heard something—just the faintest creak from outside the garage door.

I wondered if that might not happen, John thought. Little hoodlum got all the way home, then pulled his shit together and now he's come back here looking . . .

Before he could finish the thought, the whole garage rocked with a powerful boom, like a tree had fallen on the roof, or a car had come up the driveway and run into the door.

"What the hell?" John growled as he slammed the lid of the chest shut and leapt to his feet. He imagined Chad outside the place using a sledgehammer on his wall. "If you damage this house, you little bastard, you're going to discover a new definition of the word sorry!"

John yanked open the door and charged out into the walkway. Whatever that boy was doing, he was going to put a stop to it, and if he caught Chad vandalizing the place red-handed, he wouldn't need any Krampus disguise. He'd just call the police and have the kid arrested. He still had connections on the force; he knew how to make things happen.

But when John came around the front of the garage to the driveway, there was no one there to be seen. Just the distasteful display of face-down Santa and his eight horny reindeer.

John looked around in confusion for a moment, wondering just what on earth had happened to shake his garage to its foundation.

Whatever had caused that tremor, it had even displaced Santa from his resting place in the snow bank. Looking carefully for any clues, John noticed something lying in Santa's impression in the snow. He stepped closer and was surprised by a familiar sight: a greeting card with a drawing of a black, curly-tongued devil man and three words: Gruss vom Krampus.

How the hell did that get underneath his defaced Christmas ornaments? It had been a lot of years since John had seen one of those.

As he pondered, he heard another noise from behind the garage, the sound of one of his trash cans tumbling end over end. "That's enough!" he threatened as he rushed along the walk and into the back yard, ready to grab whoever was there.

John rounded the corner and came to a stop. In the dark yard, the only things John could see were two glowing little stars that had come peeking out from behind the clouds. Then he realized that the two shining points of light he was looking at weren't stars, and they weren't in the sky. They were suspended up in the air above him against something that looked like a big, dark wall.

Suddenly a gust of air, hot, fetid, and damp, washed over his face. Then the dark wall he'd nearly collided with shifted, and John saw it outlined against the cloudy night sky: long curling horns; dull, red eyes; and a mouth full of carnivorous fangs.

A flicker of disbelief passed through John's thoughts. This had to be a fake, a hoax, just another prank. Except the thing was so goddamned big. That butcher-shop reek coming off of it wasn't something you bought at a costume shop.

John heard the thing take in a rumbling, ragged breath of air that seemed to stretch on for a dozen heartbeats, like it was filling lungs the size of propane tanks. And finally, its inhalation complete, the thing spoke in a voice thick with mucous and teeth:

"John Nast," it rumbled.

Reason tied to assert itself in John's mind. Whoever or whatever this thing was, it knew his name. There had to be a logical explanation.

But the last thread of rational thought snapped when he heard the clanking of chains.

The dark shape came at him with a ponderous, malevolent gait, and suddenly his grandfather's words, as harsh and frightening as the first time he'd spoken them, came to John's mind, "Das Krampus vill come for you!"

Without so much as a willful impulse, John's feet turned and started to flee toward the house, leaving the black, hulking figure behind him. As he reached for the patio door, however, John heard another jangling sound along with a wicked hiss of air being forcibly parted. The night exploded in a flash of white pain as a link of heavy chain collided with the back of his head like a wrecking ball. The impact sent John toppling away from the door and out onto the snowy back lawn.

The familiar pain of a blow to the head helped him clear his mind. He wasn't a goddamned frightened little eight-year-old listening to his grandpa's ghost stories. He'd been doing this sort of thing all his life. He'd absorbed more than his share of punches, and he wasn't afraid to go to the pavement. Pull it together, Officer Nast!

John wiped the snow away from his face and rolled off the ground. He was halfway back up on his feet when the shape loomed over him again, raised one of its legs, and planted its sharp-clawed foot right in the middle of John's chest.

John was astonished at its massive weight. And as it leaned down to glare at him like a lion over a gored gazelle, John thought his ribcage was going to collapse. Its face was so close that John could see its pale, glassy eyes looking pitilessly into his face. This was exactly the Krampus that he had seen in his young, frightened mind when Grandpa Nast first described the devil-man.

The Krampus's horns seemed to dance in the air as it gave its furry head a shake. "You have summoned me, John Nast," it growled.

Struggling to breathe, pinned to the ground under its weight, John could barely do more than squeak like a child. "I haven't . . . summoned . . ."

"I have been summoned!" The thing's voice roared like a jet engine. "On this night of the year, I am drawn to those in need of punishment. Corruption lures me, with the foul scent of hypocrisy and dissembling. I hunt those who commit the vilest offense, passing judgment on others without standing to be judged themselves."

"But I haven't . . ." John gulped hard and squirmed under the weight of the thing's foot, trying to draw in enough breath to explain himself. "I didn't hurt that boy. I just wanted to scare him. A little. Just to get him back on the right track."

"Your list of grievances is long, John Nast," the Krampus growled. "But I have not come to settle old scores. You have wrongly punished the innocent in the guise of righteousness. The most arrogant transgression of all."

"That boy?" John sputtered. "Ain't . . . innocent! Look! You see what he did? He deserves punishment!"

The voice of the Krampus rumbled through his bones. "You reek of sanctimony and prejudice. You are tainted by the guilt that you've sought to smear upon others. And thus, I will do to you what I do to all those so tainted."

The monster straightened and lifted his foot from John's chest, and he was finally able to fill his compressed lungs. He gasped and choked as twinkling spots wiggled along the periphery of his sight. Though he hardly felt like his legs would support him, John struggled to his feet and started to move toward the back door of the house.

But the lack of air was affecting his balance, his judgment, and his coordination. John bumped into a patio chair, fell against the barbecue, and went stumbling to the far edge of the porch.

The Krampus bared its fangs at John again. "I will cleanse the offense from you. I will purge you of your vices at last."

With incredible speed the thing drew back its arm and sent the length of chain in its grip lashing forward like a whip. The blow caught John on the head again and sent him reeling, scattering plastic furniture and potted plants in every direction.

With no strength left, John let himself collapse to the ground. Whether this thing would kill him or not, he didn't know, but both his breath and his will to struggle were gone. His head pounded from the beating he'd taken by its chain. He was accustomed to being the intimidator, not the one being intimidated. He had no idea what to do, other than to plead through his tears like a helpless child.

John felt himself being lifted roughly and thrown over the monster's hairy shoulder. Step by jarring step it moved, carrying him past the garage and out to the front of the house, to the sidewalk beside River Street.

And at the edge of the walk the Krampus stopped. It lifted John like a rag doll, gave him one last, agonizing squeeze, and dropped him.

He hit the surface of what should have been hard, unyielding pavement and was surprised that instead of a thud, he landed with a splash. What little breath he had been able to recapture shot out of him again as he submerged beneath the surface of black, icy water.

Ripples spread out in every direction as John paddled helplessly, trying to reach the shore, to get to the sidewalk, to his home. But the Krampus had beaten all the strength out of him. There was nothing left to do but be pulled down into the deep, icy depths of River Street.

The Krampus stood watching in front of John's house, with all the overturned Christmas decorations behind it. That's strange, John thought, as he heard the monster's final words:

"John, can you hear me?"

* * *

John reached up slowly and rubbed the lump on his head.

"John, can you hear me?" a voice said. "Now try not to move too fast. Are you hurt?"

John opened his eyes. He recognized the rafters of his garage workshop. He recognized the jumble of storage boxes around him that had toppled off of the workbench.

And he recognized the face of the man kneeling over him: Arnold Brooks, Chad's father.

"Wh . . ." John blinked, trying to clear the confusion from his mind. "What are you doing here, Brooks?" he asked.

"Chad came and got me," Arnold explained. "He told me all about what happened."

"He did?" John asked. That wasn't too good, considering that he was surrounded by a small avalanche of old police equipment. Going to be a little hard to deny attacking a boy with a Taser when his duty belt and uniform hat were on the floor beside him.

Arnold nodded. "Chad said he came down here to explain what had happened, but you were too upset to listen. So I figured it was time for me to set things straight."

Okay, maybe the kid hadn't ratted him out. Best not to reveal anything else. John nodded a little and let Arnold go on talking.

"Guess you don't remember me, do you John?" Arnold asked.

"Uhn," John said with a gentle shake of his head. "Arnold? Live down the street? Didn't take that much of a knock on the melon, did I?"

John saw frustration, and a little contempt, come over Arnold's face. "About 20 years ago, I was in a car with some of my friends. We got pulled over on the highway by the police. We were going a little faster than we should've been, and the kid who was driving was a bit of a smart-mouth to the cop who came up to the window. So the police pulled us all out, put us into the back of a couple of patrol cars, and took us off to some dark stretch of road." Arnold gave John a questioning nod. "You know what I'm talking about?"

"I'm not sure," John hedged.

"You were there, John," Arnold said. "You threatened me and all of my friends. You roughed us up and scared the hell out of us. And you and those other officers made sure there was no possible way we could pin any of it on you. Sound about right?"

"Yeah, I guess," John said as the pounding pain in his skull slowly began to recede to a mild ache.

"That night is the reason I went to law school," Arnold said. "It's why I became a defense attorney. I swore I'd work for real justice, and fight against that sort of abuse."

"And what?" John asked. "You telling me you followed me since then? Been stalking me all that time, or something, to get some sort of revenge?"

Arnold shook his head. "No, finding you was just a coincidence, John," he said. "When Kate and I came to the open house, I looked down the street and saw you out front of this place raking leaves." He shrugged coldly. "But I wasn't completely sure until the first time I saw the Christmas decorations in your yard. The stockings on the side of that sleigh."

"My Maggie's Christmas stocking?" John asked, wondering just what that had to do with it.

"I remembered seeing a photograph on the dashboard of your police car, while I was in the back seat. 'Come home safely,' or something like that. It was signed Maggie." Arnold shook his head with a scowl. "Thinking of you with a family, living comfortably, happily. Seemed like it was a mockery of the good I was trying to do. It made me a little crazy. I decided I was going to buy that house no matter what, and then make you really sorry for what you'd done to me all those years ago."

"You?" John said. "It was you that did all that?"

"Yes, all that," he explained. All the pranks and vandalism, all the harassment and damage, it had all been done by Arnold Brooks himself. "Make no mistake, John. I wasn't proud of it. Lots of times I flat out hated myself for the petty, juvenile way I was acting."

"Not that boy of yours?" John asked.

"No," Arnold said with a note of shame. "I hate to imagine what he thought his old man was up to. I could tell he had his suspicions. Earlier tonight Chad found that stocking, the one I took with your wife's name on it, in my basement, and he put the clues together."

"He did?" John wondered.

"That's why he came over here earlier," Arnold said. "He was going to bring it back to you. My son. He was just trying to patch things up." As he thought about that, John saw the anger draining out of Arnold's face. He looked sad, on the verge of tears. "I've got to say he was a damned sight more mature than his father."

Bewildered by his own misunderstanding, John asked, "He came to return my Maggie's Christmas stocking? And he said I was just . . . angry?"

Arnold nodded. "That's right. So he came home and confronted me with it. Made me feel, well, like a damned fool. I realized I'd taken things way too far. So I came back here to make amends. And I guess it's a good thing I did, because as I walked up I heard the crash in your workshop. I looked in here and saw that your storage boxes had fallen off the bench and knocked you clean out. Lying here on the garage floor, John, unconscious in the middle of December. You could have frozen to death."

John put a hand on the workbench as he lifted himself off the concrete. "You, uh, didn't see anything else as you came in, did you Brooks?"

Arnold shrugged. "Just you and the . . . well, what's in the front yard there." He peered at John. "It's awful dark outside. Is there something else I should have seen?"

John shook his head. "Nah. Just remembering something. An old Christmas story my granddad told me years ago."

"Christmas," Arnold said as he replaced the lids on the toppled boxes and stacked them on John's workbench. "Well, in the spirit of Christmas, I decided it was time to come over here and set things right.

I've been living with a demon since that night, and I tried to blame you for putting that demon inside me. But tonight I realized that I was the one who'd become a demon. Only one responsible for the ugly, spiteful way I was acting was me, not you. And there's only one way to make a demon like that go away."

"Whazzat?" John asked.

The muscles along Arnold's jawline tightened as he stared straight into John's eyes. For a long time he didn't speak, and when he turned and moved toward side door, John thought that maybe he was going to leave without saying anything more.

Then Arnold stopped himself with a hand on the doorframe, turned to look at John over his shoulder, and said, "I forgive you, John. You haven't apologized for what you did to me, probably to a lot of others. I don't know if you even feel sorry for any of it. But I forgive you nonetheless. I forgive you because forgiving is the only way to banish a demon."

John watched Arnold closely. He recognized how much of a struggle the man went through to get those words out.

"Maybe it's time we forgive each other, Brooks," John suggested. "If you been fighting your own demons, I do regret whatever part I had in putting them there. And I suppose I did deserve a little taste of my own medicine," he added, imagining himself cringing feebly before the terrible vision of the Krampus, just as he'd once forced Arnold to do, cuffed and nearly naked on a deserted stretch of highway.

John offered his hand. Arnold, after a reluctant pause, reached out and took it. "You give your boy Chad my thanks for . . . well, for what he told you about tonight. He'll know what I mean."

"Speaking of him," Arnold said, "let me finish what he came over here to do."

Reaching into his hip pocket, Arnold brought out a neatly rolled Christmas stocking with "Maggie" written along the cuff.

* * *

Arnold and Chad were both at John's front door promptly at 6 a.m. the following morning. By the time the neighbors were out of bed, there was no trace at all of the devastation that had been wrought with John's front-yard Christmas decorations. Santa was returned to his upright position with his robe settled around him in a dignified manner. The reindeer were reassembled two by two across the lawn, harnessed in the traces of the bright red sleigh with a pair of stockings draped over its edge.

A little Christmas tableau with almost nothing to spoil its quaint charm. Almost nothing. But some people who stopped along the walk on River Street to admire the cheery scene might have noticed a strange little card lodged within branches atop Santa's staff of holly. Peering closely, they might have wondered at the wild, grotesque image of a snarling demon with sharp horns and a curled tongue drawn on that card. And, at a time when every window and storefront seemed blazoned with sentiments like "Merry Christmas" or "Happy Holidays," they might have read, with just a little curiosity, the words on that card that conveyed a different spirit of the season in the homes, and the hearts, of John Nast and his neighbor Arnold Brooks:

Gruss vom Krampus.

* * *

Scott Farrell is an author, performer, and educator, and his writing (fiction and non-fiction) has appeared in the books *Steampunk Shakespeare, Martial Arts And Philosophy*, and *Living A Life Of Value*, as well as in dozens of print and on-line publications around the world, including *The New York Times* and "Blogging Shakespeare" the official blog of the Shakespeare Birthplace Trust. He performs regularly with the educational tour program of the Intrepid Shakespeare Company, and he is the founder and director of the Chivalry Today Educational Program; Scott also teaches weekly classes in historical sword combat at two fencing academies in San Diego, Calif., where he lives with his wife, April. Discover more of Scott's work at his Facebook page, "Scott Farrell - Author," or his website, www.ScottFarrellAuthor.com.

About the Editor

Kate Wolford is editor and publisher of Enchanted Conversation: A Fairy Tale Magazine at fairytalemagazine.com. She teaches first-year college writing, incorporating fairy tales in her assignments whenever possible. Her book *Beyond the Glass Slipper: Ten Neglected Fairy Tales To Fall In Love With* is available from World Weaver Press.

BEYOND THE GLASS SLIPPER

Ten Neglected Fairy Tales To Fall In Love With
Introduction and Annotations by Kate Wolford

Some fairy tales everyone knows—these aren't those tales. These are tales of kings who get deposed and pigs who get married. These are ten tales, much neglected. Editor of *Enchanted Conversation: A Fairy Tale Magazine*, Kate Wolford, introduces and annotates each tale in a manner that won't leave novices of fairy tale studies lost in the woods to grandmother's house, yet with a depth of research and a delight in posing intriguing puzzles that will cause folklorists and savvy readers to find this collection a delicious new delicacy.

Beyond the Glass Slipper is about more than just reading fairy tales—it's about connecting to them. It's about thinking of the fairy tale as a precursor to *Saturday Night Live* as much as it is to any princess-movie franchise: the tales within these pages abound with outrageous spectacle and absurdist vignettes, ripe with humor that pokes fun at ourselves and our society.

Never stuffy or pedantic, Kate Wolford proves she's the college professor you always wish you had: smart, nurturing, and plugged into pop culture. Wolford invites us into a discussion of how these tales fit into our modern cinematic lives and connect the larger body of fairy tales, then asks—no, *insists*—that we create our own theories and connections. A thinking man's first step into an ocean of little known folklore.

FAE

An Anthology of Fairies
Edited by Rhonda Parrish

Meet Robin Goodfellow as you've never seen before, watch damsels in distress rescue themselves, get swept away with the selkies and enjoy tales of hobs, green men, pixies and phookas. One thing is for certain, these are not your grandmother's fairy tales.

Fairies have been both mischievous and malignant creatures throughout history. They've dwelt in forests, collected teeth or crafted shoes. *Fae* is full of stories that honor that rich history while exploring new and interesting takes on the fair folk from castles to computer technologies to modern midwifing, the Old World to Indianapolis.

Fae bridges traditional and modern styles, from the familiar feeling of a good old-fashioned fairy tale to urban fantasy and horror with a fae twist. This anthology covers a vast swath of the fairy story spectrum, making the old new and exploring lush settings with beautiful prose and complex characters.

FAR ORBIT

Speculative Space Adventures
Edited by Bascomb James

Modern space adventures crafted by a new generation of Grand Tradition science fiction writers. Smart and engaging stories that take us back to a time when science fiction was fun and informative, pithy and piquant—when speculative fiction transported us from the everyday grind and left us wondrously satisfied. Showcasing the breadth of Grand Tradition stories, from 1940s-style pulp to realistic hard SF, from noir and horror SF to spaceships, alien uplift, and action-adventure motifs, Far Orbit's diversity of Grand Tradition stories makes it easy for every SF fan to find a favorite.

Featuring an open letter to SF by Elizabeth Bear and stories from Gregory Benford, Tracy Canfield, Eric Choi, Barbara Davies, Jakob Drud, Julie Frost, David Wesley Hill, K. G. Jewell, Sam Kepfield, Kat Otis, Jonathan Shipley, Wendy Sparrow, and Peter Wood

"Daring adventure, protagonists who think on their feet, and out of this world excitement! Welcome to FAR ORBIT, a fine collection of stories in the best SF tradition. Strap in and enjoy!"

—Julie E. Czerneda, author of *Species Imperative*

"Successfully captures the kinds of stories that were the gateway drugs for many of us who have been reading science fiction for a long time. Well done!"

—*Tangent*

SPECTER SPECTACULAR

13 Ghostly Tales
Edited by Eileen Wiedbrauk

Once you cross the grave into this world of fantasy and fright, you may find there's no way back.

SPECTER SPECTACULAR II

13 Deathly Tales (Coming Soon)
Edited by Eileen Wiedbrauk

WOLVES AND WITCHES

A Fairy Tale Collection
Amanda C. Davis and Megan Engelhardt

Witches have stories too. So do mermaids, millers' daughters, princes (charming or otherwise), even big bad wolves.

THE KING OF ASH AND BONES

Breathtaking four-story collection
Rebecca Roland

SHARDS OF HISTORY

a fantasy novel by
Rebecca Roland

Malia fears the fierce, winged creatures known as Jeguduns who live in the cliffs surrounding her valley. But when she discovers an injured Jegudun, Malia's very existence—her status as clan mother in training, her marriage, her very life in the Taakwa village—is threatened by her choice to befriend the intelligent creature. But will anyone believe her when she learns the truth: the threat to her people is much bigger and much more malicious than the Jeguduns. Lurking on the edge of the valley is an Outsider army seeking to plunder and destroy her people, and it's only a matter of time before the Outsiders find a way through the magic shield that protects the valley—a magic that can only be created by Taakwa and Jeguduns working together.

"A must for any fantasy reader."
 —*Plasma Frequency Magazine*

"Fast-paced, high-stakes drama in a fresh fantasy world. Rebecca Roland is a newcomer to watch!"
 —James Maxey, author of *Greatshadow: The Dragon Apocalypse.*

"One of the most beautifully written novels I have ever read. Suspenseful, entrapping, and simply . . . well, let's just say that *Shards of History* reminds us of why we love books in the first place. *Five out of five stars!*"
 —Good Choice Reading

Available in ebook and paperback now.

White as snow, stained with blood,
her talons black as ebony . . .

OPAL

a novella by
Kristina Wojtaszek

The daughter of an owl, forced into human shape . . .

"A fairy tale within a fairy tale within a fairy tale—the narratives fit together like interlocking pieces of a puzzle, beautifully told."
  —Zachary Petit, Editor *Writer's Digest*

In this retwisting of the classic Snow White tale, the daughter of an owl is forced into human shape by a wizard who's come to guide her from her wintry tundra home down to the colorful world of men and Fae, and the father she's never known. She struggles with her human shape and grieves for her dead mother—a mother whose past she must unravel if men and Fae are to live peacefully together.

"Twists and turns and surprises that kept me up well into the night. Fantasy and fairy tale lovers will eat this up and be left wanting more!"
  —Kate Wolford, Editor, *Enchanted Conversation Magazine*

Available in ebook and paperback now.

ALSO FROM WORLD WEAVER PRESS

Wolves and Witches
A Fairy Tale Collection
Amanda C. Davis and Megan Engelhardt

Beyond the Glass Slipper
Ten Neglected Fairy Tales to Fall In Love With
Some fairy tales everyone knows—these aren't those tales.
Edited by Kate Wolford

The King of Ash and Bones
Breathtaking four-story collection
Rebecca Roland

The Haunted Housewives of Allister, Alabama
Cleo Tidwell Paranormal Mystery, Book One
*Who knew one gaudy Velvet Elvis
could lead to such a heap of haunted trouble?*
Susan Abel Sullivan

The Weredog Whisperer
Cleo Tidwell Paranormal Mystery, Book Two
*The Tidwells are supposed to be on spring break on the Florida Gulf Coast,
not up to their eyeballs in paranormal hijinks . . . again.*
Susan Abel Sullivan

Heir to the Lamp
Genie Chronicles, Book One (YA)
*A family secret, a mysterious lamp,
a dangerous Order with the mad desire to possess both.*
Michelle Lowery Combs

Glamour
Stealing the life she's always wanted is as easy as casting a spell.
Andrea Janes

Forged by Fate
Fate of the Gods, Book One
After Adam Fell, God made Eve to Protect the World.
Amalia Dillin

Fate Forgotten
Fate of the Gods, Book Two
To win the world, Adam will defy the gods,
but his fate rests in Eve's hands.
Amalia Dillin

Beyond Fate
Fate of the Gods, Book Three
The stunning conclusion to the Fate of the Gods trilogy.
Amalia Dillin

Tempting Fate
Fate of the Gods Novella, #1.5
Mia's lived in her sister's shadow long enough.
Amalia Dillin

The Devil in Midwinter
Paranormal romance (NA)
A handsome stranger, a terrifying monster, a boy who burns and burns . . .
Elise Forier Edie

Cursed: Wickedly Fun Stories
Collection
"Quirky, clever, and just a little savage." —*Lane Robins, critically
acclaimed author of MALEDICTE and KINGS AND ASSASSINS*
Susan Abel Sullivan

A Winter's Enchantment
Three novellas of winter magic and loves lost and regained.
Experience the magic of the seson.
Elise Forier Edie, Amalia Dillin, Kristina Wojatszek

Legally Undead
Vampirachy, Book One—*Coming May 2014*
*A reluctant vampire hunter, stalking New York City
as only a scorned bride can.*
Margo Bond Collins

Blood Chimera
Blood Chimera, Book One
Some ransoms aren't meant to be paid.
Jenn Lyons

Blood Sin
Blood Chimera, Book Two
Everything is permitted . . . and everyone has their price.
Jenn Lyons

For more on these and other titles visit WorldWeaverPress.com

WORLD WEAVER PRESS

Publishing fantasy, paranormal, and science fiction.
We believe in great storytelling.

Made in the USA
Lexington, KY
20 January 2015